Christopher, John
    Beyond the burning lands.   Macmillan
[1971]
    170 p.

Beyond the Burning Lands

Beyond the Burning Lands

by John Christopher

The Macmillan Company
New York, New York

Anatomy of Wonder, poor condition w/o Pyk series

To Liz,
with love

CONTENTS

Beyond
the Burning
Lands

ONE

Out of
Sanctuary

The Sanctuary itself lay in empty downland; ordinary men did not dare approach such a holy place. The nearest habitation was at Amesbury in the Avon Valley, three miles to the east, and it was there that the white horses were kept, on which the High Seers, when they had reason to travel abroad, would ride forth. The horses were housed in the stables of the Seer of Amesbury, who at the proper time gave orders to the grooms to have them saddled and made ready for the journey.

To the townspeople this was evidence of the magic of the Spirits which was at the Seer's command. For how, except by magic, could the Seer of Amesbury know when the High Seers required their mounts? No messenger had come across the empty land to the west, and the Seer had no pigeons

Plainly the Spirits had brought him word in the hushed darkness of the Seance Hall where the Seer and his Acolytes conducted their devotions.

Such was the townspeople's belief and the Seers were happy to encourage it. In fact communication was by radio. The main transmitter was underground in the Sanctuary, with a cunningly concealed wire leading to an aerial on top of one of the huge monoliths that stood in a broken circle above The subsidiary set was in a heavily locked room in the Seer's House to which only the Seer and his chief Acolyte had the key. Because radios, of course, were machines, and machines were forbidden by the Spirits, anyone building or using one was punishable by death. This was by the command of the Seers themselves.

My initial shock at learning the truth about the Seers had been great, but during the months in which I had lived in the Sanctuary I had grown accustomed to it. I had come there from Winchester where, following my father's treacherous murder by the Prince of Romsey, my half-brother Peter had won back the city and claimed the title of Prince. It was I, Luke, who, though younger, had been my father's heir, named as Prince in Waiting by the Spirits and promised great glory when the time came for me to rule. The blow of learning that the Spirits, since they did not exist, could not keep their promises had been bitter. Instead the High Seers unfolded what was, they said, a higher mission.

We lived in the ruins of a world that had once been great. Men thought our ancestors had shattered the planet with the machines which were now forbidden. This was not so. The disaster that took place had been a natural one. The earth had heaved itself up in earthquakes and volcanoes and at the same time the sun had poured forth radiations which altered the pattern of living things, creating strange plants and animals—polybeasts—and often causing men and women to be born misshapen. In civilized lands beasts and plants were destroyed if they did not breed true. Human children were permitted to live but, if they were not true men, were called dwarf or polymuf. The dwarfs were a breed apart and respected as craftsmen. Polymufs might have any manner of deformity; they lived as servants and could hold no property.

Spiritism had sprung up in the dark days after the world crashed into ruins. Those who survived had turned against machines, and the science which had produced them, thinking them responsible for the Disaster. The Seers had taken over the trappings of Spiritism, finding men's belief in the Spirits and in the strange happenings that took place in the darkened Seance Halls a useful means of controlling them, and the revulsion against machines was part of this. For the present it had to be accepted.

But the time in which a change might be made was growing short. Recovery even to a primitive form of civilized life had been precarious. The concentration of volcanic dust in the air made winters longer and harder, and brought more pressure from savages in outlying lands. The little which had been regained could easily be lost.

It seemed to the Seers that the first and essential need was to unite the constantly warring cities under one ruler, and through him achieve a rebirth of science and knowledge. Winchester had been chosen as the city through which this was to be accomplished, and I as the Prince who would bring it about. The Seers' plans had received a grievous setback with my father's death when I was still only fifteen and unable to enforce my claims against those of my brother. That was when Ezzard, the Seer of Winchester, had taken me from the city in disguise and brought me to the Sanctuary. While I lived, the secret aim of the Seers was still possible.

I accepted this and my part in it but with less enthusiasm than theirs. I had been reared and trained as a warrior, at first a Captain's son and then the son and heir of the Prince. My mind thought best in terms of military strategies, my hand was fitted neither for pen nor workbench but the hilt of a sword. The wonders that the High Seers showed me, of which radio was but one example, were interesting enough but a drab exchange for the life of the open air, of riding, jousting, the talk and laughter of soldiers. I knew the High Seers as men now, and liked them, but much of their converse was beyond me, and I missed the salty tang of camp and barracks.

It was because of this, and my evident and growing impatience with confinement and inactivity, that an extra white horse was saddled and led across the snowy plain by the Seer of Amesbury and two of his Acolytes. It was a custom of the High Seers to visit Salisbury for the Christmas Feast and hold a Seance there. (Salisbury, as the city holding theoretical title to the land in which the Sanctuary lay, had certain privileges which it jealously guarded; the Christmas visit was one of these.) This year the party would consist of four black-cloaked figures, not three.

The burly black-haired Murphy gave me warning before we left:

"There was some doubt of the wisdom of this, Luke. After all, to us ·you are a very precious possession and it makes no sense to hazard it." He smiled. "But if we keep you bottled up much longer there is a risk you may explode; so you will ride with Lanark and Tanner and me to the Salisbury Feast, as our special Acolyte. Make sure you behave with the discretion a special Acolyte can be expected to show, and that you keep a pale and holy look on your face. And at the banquet, of course, you will eat and drink very little, only enough for politeness' sake, because we High Seers live on air and the radiance of the Spirits, as all men know. We will take our dinners afterward in the Seer's House. He has a good cook and keeps a fine ale."

I promised to bear this in mind but in fact scarcely heard what he said. I was in a fever of restlessness, chafing more than ever at the restrictions of this man-made cavern. When we left I had to be restrained from leaping the stairs two or three at a time. On the top landing we had to wait while Lanark pressed the button which opened the trap door. It rose creaking above our heads. Daylight was strange and lovely after the artificial electric light, and my nostrils sniffed cold fresh air.

We went by way of Amesbury, where the people also claimed the right to see and venerate their High Seers, and then took the valley road south. Our cloaks were of heavy wool but it was still cold; snow lay thick and the river was rimmed with ice. The day was fairly clear, showing patches of blue, though the horizon at our backs was grimy with the smoke from the Burning Lands; we were much nearer to them than at Winchester, where one only saw the distant glow at night.

The winter landscape had little of interest to offer, but just to be in the open was enough. Nor was the horse such as I had been used to—it was a broad-backed, placid beast that traveled as suited the dignity of a party of Seers—but again it was a joy to be in the saddle even at this ambling pace. We took three hours to cover the twelve miles from Amesbury to the capital. The High Seers talked among themselves, and I thought of the two friends I had left behind in Winchester. Martin, as an Acolyte, would doubtless be at his books but Edmund, on an afternoon like this, was more likely to be at the tiltyard or out with his falcon after wild duck. I wondered if they still met in the place Martin and I had found under the great ruins behind the Seance Hall.

Salisbury lies where several valleys come together—I suppose that is why men built it there. Word had been sent of our coming and a crowd was gathered on the wall by the North Gate in front of it. When the High Seers came to Winchester the citizens had greeted them in awed silence, but the men of Salisbury shouted and cheered. It was a more usual thing with them, of course. They pressed close in on us as we rode through the streets, swept clear of snow by the polymufs, toward the Prince's palace, and I caught the smell of humanity: pungent, almost overpowering after the filtered air of the Sanctuary, but also exciting. My father had been born a commoner and promoted to Captain's rank on the field of battle. I myself had never been truly at ease with the mob, but I was glad now to see them, even to smell their rankness. I would have liked to respond to their cries and cheers; but I remembered what I was supposed to be and kept my eyes down and my lips tight shut.

Prince Harold came out of his palace to pay his respects and himself held the reins of Lanark's horse while he dismounted. This Prince was a thin dark man who had gained a reputation as a warrior in the past but for some years had been in poor health. Even while addressing the High Seers he was forced to break off by a fit of coughing, and I noticed that the linen he put to his lips came away with its whiteness stained red with blood. His two sons were also present, deferentially in the background. It would not be long, the Seers had said, before one of them ruled in his place. They were planning for the Spirits to proclaim the younger, who had proved more amenable to their guidance.

From the palace we went to the Seer's House where we were to lodge. The Prince had made formal offer of hospitality and had been formally refused. The High Seers were too holy to mix closely with ordinary men; and the arrangements for dining would have been difficult also. In the Seer's House there were no polymuf servants: the Acolytes looked after us. We were given a substantial supper. If the populace could have seen Murphy, as I did, tucking into a third helping of game pie they might have cheered on a different note. I did not do badly myself and the ale, as he had promised, was excellent.

Afterward they sat and talked. I was soon bored by it. Lanark, noticing this, said:

"Fresh air is tiring, Luke. And tomorrow will be a long day, with the ceremonies and the Seance and the banquet at night. You should get to bed. We don't want our special Acolyte yawning while we are summoning the Spirits."

I said good night readily enough and went to the room which had been prepared for me. It was a small one on the first floor, normally belonging to one of the trainee Acolytes who I suppose had been made to double up with another for the period of our stay. It held, apart from the narrow bed, a chair and small table, a cupboard and a very roughly made chest of drawers—our joiner dwarfs in Winchester would have been ashamed to turn out anything of so poor a quality.

There was nothing to do here except go to bed—the only book I found was a standard work of Seance rituals —but my tiredness had left me as soon as I got away from the High Seers and their talk of science-this and science-that. Carrying the oil lamp I explored the prospects offered by the cupboard and chest of drawers. The former was empty and so were the two top drawers of the latter. There was something in the bottom drawer but only clothing. I put the lamp down. There were woolen pants and tunic, the pants red, the tunic blue and gray. Not Acolyte clothes, which like those of the Seers were black. They were most likely the dress in which the trainee had come to the Seer's House, kept here until he passed his first apprenticeship and made his vows.

I measured the pants against my legs. They fitted well; the Acolyte, whoever he was, must be about my height. I wondered if he had accustomed himself yet to the somber garb of his calling: I felt sure I would not in fifty years. I had no fondness for those who peacocked about in scarves and gaudy trappings, but a warrior needed some color about him.

My eye caught a flare of light through the small square window to the right of the chest of drawers. I looked out to see what it was. Nothing much: a man (or more likely a polymuf servant) crossing the street with a torch. The room overlooked the street and stood no more than a dozen feet above it. I opened the double panes, with some difficulty. The cool night air came in and also the sounds of the city: the distant murmur of voices, a dog howling, a man singing far off.

They sounded sweet to me, these echoes of a world from which I was cut off. If I dressed myself in the pants and tunic . . . the drop into the street was nothing. And getting back? I leaned out and saw a drainpipe within reach. It should not be too difficult.

My enthusiasm was checked by a gust of breeze, cold against my skull. We had all cropped our heads before leaving the Sanctuary, and this would mark me even more plainly than the black dress. An Acolyte wandering the streets at night: it was unthinkable.

Reluctantly I returned the pants to the drawer, but as I did so I moved the tunic and saw something beneath it. It was a woolen balaclava, red with a blue pompom. It would cover the whole top of my head and much of my face. I pulled it on and twisted it into place. The fit was warm and snug. I stepped into the trousers and tied the waist with a cord. The tunic completed the outfit, buttoning over the top of the pants and the bottom of the balaclava. I would have liked to check my appearance in a mirror but since there was none available I had to make do with an inspection of what I could see of myself directly. It looked all right. The tunic was a little tight, but that would not be unusual on a lad whose parents' purse found it hard to keep pace with his growing.

The sill was deep. I climbed up into it and balanced there crouching for a moment. Then I dropped down into the street.

It was a quiet spot, as was usually the case in areas surrounding a Seer's House. I walked off quickly toward the sounds I had heard and a glow of light. I came after a few minutes into one of the main streets of the city. It was busier than normal since this was the eve of the Christmas Feast. Extra oil lamps had been set up on poles and people strolled and chatted through the pools of light and the darker places between. They were mostly going one way and I followed the stream. The street turned a corner and opened into a square set up with booths. There were still more lamps, each stall having at least one, and a great crowd of people.

This would be where the Beast Fair was held; in fact at the end there were cattle still on show and men bidding for them. But there were also stalls selling food and drink —sweet cakes and toddies poured into small pewter pots from steaming tureens—and toys and trinkets and fir trees for the Christmas Feast; and others where one played games to win prizes. Or hoped to win: the odds were very much against the player. There were a couple of tents with men waiting outside for admission. In one, it seemed, there would be wrestling matches, and in the other girls dancing to music and minstrels and jugglers.

I had no money in my pocket and so could not buy anything, but I did not mind. It was enough to listen to the cries of the hucksters, the hum and laughter of the crowd, the thin hiss of the naphtha lamps. At one stall a man had puppies for sale. They whined when he picked them up and a woman upbraided him for his clumsiness. So he lifted another, a ball of golden-brown fur, and it howled louder than the rest, and I watched him sell it to her for five shillings, which was much more than was reasonable.

After the months of confinement everything was interesting. I reached another tent and, peering in at the entrance, saw that it had been set up as a tavern. Potmen served drinks from behind trestle tables and there were benches at which men sat. Braziers glowed red with coals. The men were talking and laughing, their faces crimson like the stoves. They would be singing soon.

I was about to move away when a hand clamped on my arm from behind. I turned quickly to see a man in sheepskin coat, square black hat and shining gaiters: a farmer, probably, and one who looked prosperous. He said:

"If you're seeking a pot of ale, lad, enter and get it. Don't block the road for thirstier men."

I said: "I was just going, sir."

"A draft of mulled ale will warm your heart on a night like this." I shook my head. "Then in that case what were you up to, Tom-peeping in?"

I was anxious to get away from him and even more anxious not to raise suspicions. I said:

"I was looking for my father, but he is not there."

"Have you looked properly?" I nodded. 'Then come inside and wait. You are as likely to find him by staying as by wandering around. A drink will do you good."

I tried to pull away but he had me fast. I said: "I came without money . . ."

"Then you are lucky that I am in a different case! I've sold five cows today and for once I have no complaint about the price." With his free hand he jingled coins in his pocket. "You will drink with me till your father comes, and then if he wishes he can buy me a pot in return. And if not, no matter. The Spirits would not look with favor on any man who showed a hard heart on the eve of the Christmas Feast."

I said: "Thank you, sir. But I must . . ."

He pushed me ahead of him through the entrance to the tent and steered me to a table at the center. I realized that this was not the first tavern he had visited since he sold his cows. He shouted for mulled ale—a pint for him and a gill for me. There were others round us and he was between me and the entrance. For the moment there was nothing I could do.

I expected questions: who I was, where I lived, all natural enough but things to which I might find difficulty in making safe answer. To my relief, after he had seen me take my first sip of the hot spiced ale, he turned his attention to other men sitting at the table. They were talking of some scandal involving a Captain of the Prince's guard, and my farmer had much to say and loudly. I sat quiet beside him. When I had finished my gill, I would slip away. He was so engrossed that he perhaps would not notice my going.

Concerned with this and not much interested in local gossip, I did not at first realize that the conversation had changed. I was made aware of it when my companion declared, loudly enough to make me sit up despite the wool over my ears:

"That I don't believe! No one can cross the Burning Lands. Whoever says so is a liar."

"But he that told me saw the man himself."

It was a thin, leathery old fellow who spoke, a veteran judging by the scar that ran down one cheek. The farmer said:

"And knew it was so, I warrant, by the flames that came out of his boots and the cinders in his beard!"

The veteran said stubbornly: "There is a pass. It lies due north of Marlborough." This was a town in Oxford's territory and lying nearest to the Burning Lands. "He had to go through hot ash, he said, and he did indeed singe his boots with it. But he came through. His city lies far to the north, beyond savage places."

"He tells a good tale," the farmer said. "But there have always been liars and the world will never run short of fools to believe them."

He laughed and so did others. The thin man said:

"The one who told me fought at my side through a score of campaigns. No liar and no fool." He rose to his feet and stared at the farmer. "Do you say he is, friend?"

At our table there was sudden quiet. The veteran might be fifteen years older than the farmer and scarcely more than half his size, but his voice had a honed edge of menace. The farmer laughed again but with less ease.

"I say it is time we had another drink! All of us. You

too, old soldier." He waved to the potman. "And I will pay the round. And one for your comrade, if he comes in, and one for the traveler from beyond the Burning Lands!"

He was doing his best to pass it off as a joke but I knew, as all there did, that he was backing down from fear of an older and smaller man. The veteran said nothing but kept his cold gaze on him. The farmer said:

"By the Great, it's hot in here!" He undid his coat. "I am sweating like a pig. And look at this lad!" He wished, I realized, to turn attention from himself. "Sitting there stewing in a balaclava. Take it off, boy, and be at your ease."

"No, sir," I said. "I do not—"

"I say you shall!" He had found someone he could safely bully and was not to be thwarted. His hand tugged open my tunic top and grasped the bottom of the balaclava. I tried to prevent him but he did not want for strength nor against a boy off the streets, courage. He ripped the woolen helmet roughly up over my face and head.

I heard a shocked murmur as my shaved head was exposed. The farmer said:

"What have we here?" Disgust and triumph were both present in his voice. "This is a fine sight—an Acolyte in an ale tent on the eve of the Feast! We will see what the Seer says to it."

The stocks were in the open square in front of the Prince's palace. I was fastened in, legs and arms through holes in the wood, and the planks locked down. There had been a heavy frost in the night which lingered in a dank white mist. But I did not have much time to brood on being cold. A crowd had collected even before I arrived under escort, and wasted scant time in showing what it thought of an Acolyte who went from the Seer's House in disguise and supped in ale tents.

There was no shortage of rotting vegetables and similar refuse, and one would think the hens of Salisbury were trained to lay month-old eggs for this very purpose. A Sergeant stood by to make sure no stones were thrown, but a roll of stale bread, as I learned, can be hard enough. Several rapped my skull and one drew blood from my face when I did not duck fast enough.

But pain and discomfort were nothing compared with humiliation, and humiliation was overridden by hatred— not so much against the throwers as against the High Seers for allowing me to suffer such a punishment. I felt so bitter, so betrayed, that I had a mind to shout out the whole truth about them and the Sanctuary—to tell these people who mocked me that they themselves were mocked, that the Spirits were a lie and the Seances webs of trickery.

It would have done no good, of course. They would merely have thought me mad as well as wicked. There was nothing for it but to endure the jeers and the filth in silence.

At the point at which I reached this conclusion I found myself with defenders after all. A group came who by the crosses embroidered on their clothing were plainly Christians. There were half a dozen of them and they remonstrated with the ones who were pelting me with rubbish. I could just make out the drift of their argument above the din. The stocks, they declared, were an evil custom at best, but on this, the day of the birth of their Lord, it was foul blasphemy to torture another living creature.

I did not know which Lord they spoke of—I had thought

they recognized no human authority except their priests—but I welcomed the small relief from my tormentors. Small indeed; they did not waste time arguing but continued throwing. Then the Christians carried their folly further, walking out to form a screen in front of me. I felt less gratitude for this than contempt for their idiocy. No guard could stand by and tolerate such interference with an official punishment, especially one not only ordered by the Prince but asked for by the High Seers.

The Sergeant gave his orders. The Christians offered no resistance as the guard put them up also to be shied at. There was only room for three more in the stocks, so the rest were manacled hand and foot and left lying in the snow beside us. All this put the crowd in a thoroughly good humor, and with so many more targets I got off more lightly for the rest of my stay.

The Christians sang their chants all the while they were there. They were still singing when the guards released me and led me away.

It was Murphy who received me in the Seer's House. He was cold and distant in the presence of the soldiers, but said when we were left alone:

"Well, Luke, I hope they did not give you too hard a time of it."

I stared at him. I was covered with filth and my head throbbed. The cut beneath my eye was swelling. I said:

"Hard enough, sir. It is kind of you to inquire."

"Listen," he said, "you did a foolish thing in going out last night. You were caught, and punishment followed. It is something that must be accepted."

"I was brought to you. You did not need to hand me back to them, to ask to have me put in the stocks."

"No? I think we did. You are by your age plainly a trainee, too young to have taken vows and so lacking the protection of our cloth. It is essential for the common people to respect that cloth. Since you disgraced it in their eyes, it was necessary that those eyes should witness your thing. To be made sport of by the mob is another."

I said: "There are things due to me also. My father was Prince of a greater city than this. Punishment is one thing. To be made sport of by the mob is another."

"It offends your dignity?"

"I have been trained to fight," I said, "to face wounding or death, even death by execution. But not to endure the mockery of curs. I saw polymufs grinning at me."

"Your dignity is not important. That is something you have to learn."

"But the dignity of the High Seers is?"

Murphy shook his head. "No. What is important is the restoration of human order and human knowledge. Everything must serve that."

I looked at him angrily, in silence. He said:

"Remember that we made your father Prince and made you Prince in Waiting. We brought you from Winchester when there was a score of men eager to cut you down, confident that the new Prince, your brother, would thank them for it, and glad anyway to see one Perry the less. We have kept you in the Sanctuary and may yet restore you to this dignity which you prize so much."

"Yet! In what time? Five years? Ten? Fifty, perhaps?"

"Sooner, I hope." He relaxed and smiled. "How would

you like to leave the Sanctuary and go back to Winchester, Luke?"

I shook my head. "Do not mock me, sir."

"No mocking. I have a Christmas gift for you. Your brother seeks your return and pledges his word to your safety."

I said, scarcely trusting myself to believe it: "This is not a joke?"

"News came this morning while you were in the stocks. Your brother is married to a Christian, as you know. The man they say was a god was born, they also say, on this day more than twenty-two centuries ago. Perhaps she asked it of your brother; the Christians' ways are strange."

I thought of the Christians putting themselves between me and the mob. I wondered if they were still in the stocks, and still chanting.

I said: "It is really true? When do I leave?"

"You are eager to be rid of us," Murphy said. "We return to the Sanctuary tomorrow and you will leave a few days after that."

I believed it now and forgot my anger and my bruises. I forgot even the filth with which I was smeared. It was Murphy who reminded me of it. Sniffing, he said:

"A more urgent need is that you have a bath and change into clean linen. Our somber black for a while still. But because of your disgrace you will not appear at any ceremonies, nor sit solemn at the banquet. That is another good thing you get from today's misfortunes."

TWO

TOASTS
AT A BANQUET

Ezzard accompanied me on my return to Winchester. It was accepted by Peter that my life had been in danger in the days following our father's murder and his own accession, and that the Seer had been right to take me away. That was the official story, but I imagined there was more to it. Though he had married a Christian Peter himself was a Spiritist, as far as he was anything, and so also were his Captains. It was not easy even for a strong Prince to defy the Seers for long.

We went on horseback, openly, Ezzard in Seer's robes and I in clothes befitting my rank. I wore also a sword, a parting gift from the High Seers: the Sword of the Spirits which had been promised to me when they came to Winchester after the taking of Petersfield. Handing it to me, Murphy said:

"Steel, case-hardened in an induction furnace. You will find no metal to come near it, and no blade that will match it in strength and cutting edge. Look after it and it will serve you well."

We called at various towns on our way. Everywhere Ezzard let it be known that I was returning on my brother's invitation, thus binding his honor more firmly to my safety. The precaution, as he said, was probably unnecessary, but it was best to take no chances. So despite my impatience we did not hurry on the journey.

But at last, having spent the night as guests of its Prince, we left Andover in the morning and I had high hopes of reaching Winchester by night. The weather dashed these: a light fall of snow before midday turned, in the afternoon, into a driving blizzard. We had passed Headbourne Worthy, the nearest village north of the city, and had not much more than a mile to go. The distance was tantalizingly short but as the wind howled and the blinding snow drove into our faces, even I was forced to agree that we must seek shelter. We found it in a farm, where we were respectfully received and well looked after. They gave us tidings of the city, to which I listened greedily. The farmer and his wife had a son, a boy of twelve. He told me he had seen me win the Sword of Honor in the Contest, and recited a full account of it. His dream was to be a warrior, and I told him to come to me when he was of age and I would enlist him in my troop. He was deeply grateful for the promise, which I thought was likely to profit me also. He was a strong, capable lad, with the makings of a soldier.

His mother was less pleased, since he was her only son, but she would reconcile herself to losing him: she must have known he was not the sort of boy to stay on a farm once he was grown.

I had feared, when we retired to bed with the blizzard still howling, that we might be immured in the farmhouse for days. The morning dawned clear, however, the sky gray but no longer threatening, and when the servants had cut a path through drifted snow to the stable we were able to leave. Our horses floundered at times where the snow was loosely packed but we made fair progress. I saw, even in this landscape blanketed in white, landmarks I knew: Wherry's mill, a clump of fir trees that leaned in toward each other like conspirators, a rusty crumbling shaft that came from the ancient times and was shunned by children, being thought to harbor ghosts. And beyond these, so familiar and so dear, the walls of my native city. I was home again. Turning my head so that Ezzard would not see, I put up my sleeve and brushed the dampness from my eyes.

If I had any doubts of my welcome they were dispelled by the shout of joy from the guard on the North Gate. Its Sergeant, who had been in my father's troop when he was still a Captain and whom I could remember, when I was five or six, fencing with me with wooden sticks for swords, gave me the ceremonial salute, and his men yelled their heads off in acclamation. The ordinary people took up the cry and followed us through the streets as we rode to the palace. And the news must have gone ahead because when we reached the palace yard many of the Captains were assembled. I saw Greene and Meredith and Nicoll, small watchful Harding who had hoped to be Prince after my father's death, and blustering Blaine who had cuffed me into a corner when I urged them to ride against our own walls to avenge him. I saw Edmund's brother, Charles, whose father had been Prince until my father, with Ezzard's help, unseated him. And last I saw my brother, who held that title which the Spirits, through Ezzard's trickery, had promised to me: Prince of Winchester.

I dismounted and let a soldier take my horse. I walked toward Peter, my feet sinking into snow which the polymufs had not yet had time to clear away. I bowed my head and said:

"Greetings, sire."

He put a hand on my shoulder. He said, smiling:

"No ceremony between brothers! Come in, Luke, and we will drink your health."

The day of my return had been proclaimed a feast, and in the evening there was to be a banquet in celebration. Meanwhile there was the confusion of people greeting me. Some were sincere; others, I very well knew, were not. Blaine, who fulsomely gave thanks to the Spirits for protecting me, would have liked to slip a dagger between my ribs. Harding, a more wily man, would have preferred to watch him, or any other, do it. But there were those like Sergeant Burke, who looked after me on my first campaign, and Wilson, my father's most trusted comrade, whose gladness was real and unmistakable. There was also Ann, the Prince's Lady.

I had seen little of her in the old days. The estrangement between Peter and me had kept me from visiting the house in the River Road where they lived; and of course she was a Christian and so of no importance in the city.

I had known her as a quiet, perhaps simple woman, without beauty or indeed much else to explain my brother's choosing her. When I paid my respects I found she had only one woman in attendance—my mother had never had less than half a dozen. This one she dismissed, if dismissal is the right term to use of what was no more than a request, modestly put, that we might be left alone together. She said:

"Let me look at you. Have they been taking proper care of you, your High Seers? You are paler than you were. And taller. And they have shaved your head, but that will soon grow. We shall see that mop of fierce black hair again before spring."

I was surprised that she paid me such attention, or remembered me so well. And her smile surprised me with its warmth, and the way it changed a face which I had thought plain and insignificant. I made some sort of reply and she said:

"I cannot express how glad I am to see you, Luke. Not only for your sake but for Peter's. He could not be happy, knowing you were in exile and from fear of him. He would never have harmed you, and this reconciliation gladdens his heart. He has been so much happier since he asked the Seers to send you back and they agreed."

And also, I guessed, since he had done that which was pleasing to his wife's strange Christian conscience. Nor had I any doubt that the main urging for my recall had come from her. Her influence over him was plainly great and this was something to be remembered. I could not see why

it should be so—why a man should let any woman domin-
ate his mind—but the fact that one did not understand a
thing was no reason for not weighing its effects. There
would not be many things in which Peter would run
counter to her wishes.

I said: "I am glad to be back, my Lady."

She shook her head. "Call me Ann, as your sister. My
Lady is not a title I like, in any case. There is only one who
merits it—the mother of our Lord."

The Lord being, as Murphy had explained, the Christian
god. It was puzzling to think of a god with a mother but
I thought it best to ask no questions. I was not, in any
case, interested in the oddities of their religion. We talked
together for a time and kissed as brother and sister when
we parted.

I had sent messages to Edmund and Martin, saying I
would be at our usual meeting place at four of the afternoon. I got to the Ruins a little before that. I went down
the stairs and, lighting my way with a candle, through the
secret way to the hidden door and our den behind it. Inside I found an oil lamp which I lit. It was still strange not to
command the bright steady light of electricity at the flick
of a switch; the illumination from the lamp was dim and
patchy, leaving shadows in the corners. But even by its
feeble glow I could see that the place had fallen into dis-
use. Dust was thick on every surface. The chessboard was
set out with pieces and a spider had stretched its web
across them. That probably meant that Martin had been
here last. It was he who was keen on chess problems and

Edmund, in any case, would have tidied up before leaving: he could not bear disorder.

I heard footsteps. The door was pushed open and Edmund came in. He said:

"You are here before me, Luke."

We looked at each other for a moment before I put out my hand and he took it in a firm grip. I remembered that he had offered to go with me into exile, and that when I escaped instead with Ezzard I had sent him no word. But the constraint between us came from my side, not his. I had looked forward so much to seeing him but did not know what to say. I said awkwardly:

"You do not come here now?"

"Not since you left." He looked round the room. "Nor Martin, either, it would seem."

"You have not been seeing Martin?"

He shrugged. "Now and then, by chance. He is busy with his studies and I have had my own concerns."

We talked, but the awkwardness remained. I think we were both glad to hear Martin approaching. He came to me and shook hands also. Edmund began to shake with laughter. I asked him:

"What is it? A good joke?"

It took him a moment to control himself sufficiently to speak. He said, gasping:

"It was the sight of the pair of you—those two shaved heads . . ."

Martin stared at him owlishly: he had taken to wearing spectacles since I last saw him and the effect, together with the long black robe of an Acolyte, was slightly comic. I realized I must look nearly as odd, if not odder, in warrior's leather but with a naked skull, and laughed as well. Martin joined in. We stood there, the small chamber echoing with our laughter, and the feeling of strangeness and uncertainty dissolved in it.

"Thank the Great yours is only temporary," Edmund said to me, still laughing. "I would have felt truly forsaken had you both turned Acolyte. And one could not rule out the possibility, Luke, since you were living in the Sanctuary with the High Seers. They might well have talked you into it!"

"It would need a great deal of talking," I said. "And there is such a thing as aptitude. I do not think the High Seers ever fancied me as a recruit to the Order."

"They cropped your head."

"There was a reason for that."

I was on the point of saying that they had cropped their own as well before I remembered to guard my tongue. Edmund, flinging himself onto one of the chairs and sitting backward astride it, said:

"But what is it like there? Is it true that you get to the Sanctuary by climbing up a rainbow? And that you eat clouds and drink butterfly milk? What have you been doing all the time you have been away?"

Martin said quickly: "He cannot tell us about it. It is forbidden for him to tell or for us to listen."

In this same place Edmund had asked Martin, newly made an Acolyte, about the secrets he had learned and I, on his behalf, had said much the same as he was saying now. I had not guessed what secrets there might be, nor how soon I would be made privy to them. I wondered how much Martin himself knew; even with him I dared not speak freely of what I had seen.

I said: "It is all dull stuff, anyway. Tell me what has been happening here in Winchester since I've been gone."

They told me the news: how such a one had broken a leg in a fall out hunting, how another had perpetrated an elaborate jest against Blaine's son Henry and got into trouble when Blaine himself was tricked by it, how one of the Dwarf Coiners of the Prince's Mint had been found to have debased the gold but had fled before he could be punished. Who had been promoted, who fallen from favor. Who won the toboggan race which was held yearly in the High Street after the first snow. I listened with an interest whetted by the months of confinement to the duller conversation of the High Seers. Martin said:

"But the really interesting thing happened only two days ago, when the peddler came."

"The peddler?" I asked.

Edmund said: "He has goods to sell, but you could as well call him liar as peddler. He says he has come across the Burning Lands, from some city far to the north."

I nodded. "I have heard tell of him. You think he lies?"

"What else? No man can cross the Burning Lands. Peddlers always have tall tales. They are for the women, to catch their interest so that afterward they can sell them trinkets at fancy prices. It is just that this one has a taller tale than most."

"He wears strange clothes," Martin said.

"Which he claims is the garb of his native land. I could

devise something of the sort myself. With a pouch just above the waist, perhaps, for keeping rain off my head when I was carrying it under my arm!"

The men with their heads beneath their arms who would come from beyond the Burning Lands was one of the fantasies with which polymuf maids sometimes frightened naughty children. Edmund and I laughed, but Martin said:

"It is not only his clothes that are different. The things he sells are, also. I looked at a necklace which my cousin bought. The workmanship was not like any I have seen."

"There are always new fashions in necklaces," Edmund said. "It means nothing."

"But if the fires of the Burning Lands *are* dying down, and one could cross them . . ."

"One would find savages and polybeasts. What else?"

"Perhaps another city, as he says."

"In any case, who cares?" Edmund said. "There is enough to concern us in this city." He turned to me, dismissing the other topic. "Luke, I am glad to see you again. But are you safe?"

"I think so. And the High Seers would not have sent me here unless they thought the same."

"The Spirits named you, not Peter, Prince in Waiting. And promised you glory. This is something that will be remembered, and for some the memory of it will be a stink in their nostrils."

"I trust my brother. And his honor is pledged."

And his will, I thought, under the bidding of his Lady's conscience; but I did not say that. Edmund said:

"Do you know the story of Donald the Red?"

"No."

"I had it from a polymuf maid, and old woman who had been in the palace in my grandfather's day." At a time, I did not need reminding, when my grandfather was a humble carpenter with a strong son eager to exchange the adz for the sword. "He was a Captain who fought well in the campaigns and was popular with the other Captains. For two years, while our army did badly he himself scored great successes. There was talk of a plot to make him Prince, and other talk of accusing him of treason before the plot could succeed. My grandfather would have none of that, despite the urgings of his friends. But in the next campaign Red Donald was killed and it was said his wound was in the back. It was not my grandfather's doing, but the man died. Your brother might have friends of a similar mind."

This was true, and true that Ann's Christian conscience could not hold her husband guilty of a murder planned by others, a deed of which he knew nothing. I was, of course, under the special protection of the Seers; but so had my father been and it had not saved him. I said, smiling:

"Thank you for the warning! But I do not think I am in any danger."

"All the same," Edmund said, "if I were you I should keep my back well guarded."

The banquet was held in the Great Hall. I sat at the right hand of the Prince and as guest of honor drank with him from the great gold pot which had been our father's, and Prince Stephen's and Prince Egbert's before that. No women were present, of course. The Captains sat above the first salt, other dignitaries between the first and second, and lesser guests below. I saw my old friend, Rudi the Armorer Dwarf, and catching my eye from that distance he raised his pot to me in greeting.

After the last of the meats were cleared and before the sweets were brought it fell to me to give the Prince's toast. I stood and the company with me. I lifted the golden pot and gave the health of the Prince of Winchester. The cry echoed down the table, and we drank.

My brother rose as I took my seat. He said:

"I would have you drink again. This time to Luke, my brother."

Afterward he remained standing. He said:

"And I have news for you and him. Tonight I make him Captain." His raised hand quelled the murmur of surprise and applause. "He is young for the rank but already capable, and promises better. And there is something else that I would say."

I looked at him standing by me. Although I was still growing I knew I would never match his height, which was two inches over six feet. He had my father's fair hair and breadth of face and chest. The brooding expression which once had marred his features had gone, replaced by an easy smiling confidence. He was a true Prince. I wished I could feel more glad of that.

"You do not need reminding," he went on, "of certain things that have been between us, and I do not wish to dwell on them. But one is better spoken of than left hidden. There was a Seance, after my father's acclamation as Prince, in which this brother of mine was named Prince in Waiting and promised a great and glorious future. Yet I am Prince of Winchester, though named by no Spirit, and he is not."

He paused and they were silent, waiting on his words. My brother looked down at Ezzard, who sat next to him on the other side.

"As the Seer himself will tell you, the prophecies of the Spirits are not always what they seem. Luke may still have a destiny of triumph, in another city, perhaps even another land. In this city I rule, and will do so. But I say this to you: after my Lady, my brother is the most precious to me of all. I pledge myself, by my honor as Prince, by the Great Spirit, and by any other god that may be, to protect and care for him. I say this also: if harm should come to him I will hunt down the man who does it and kill him with my own hands."

There was a moment's silence before they started cheering and banging their pots. He stood there smiling. When at last the noise died down, he said:

"There will be no dissension between us brothers. By his return Luke declares this also, and renounces the claims that others made for him. So I ask him now to seal the contract as I have done. I ask him, by the Great Spirit, to pledge allegiance to me and to my heirs."

I fought to control my face against the feelings that pressed in on me. Apart from anything else I was astounded: I would not have thought he had such guile. Had the Christian priest, perhaps, counseled him? Or Ann? I could not believe it of her. I wondered what Ezzard was thinking; whatever it was he would show nothing. I forced a smile to my lips and kept it there as I rose to face the two long lines of faces. In the strongest voice I could muster, I said:

"In the name of the Great Spirit, I pledge my allegiance to Peter, Prince of Winchester, and to his heirs."

They cheered at that, though I thought the face of Blaine, who sat a little way down the table, showed puzzlement: his eyes in their folds of fat were narrowed. Harding, sitting opposite, was impassive as always.

My brother put his hand on my shoulder. I felt its weight as strong, oppressive, and would have liked to shake it off. He said:

"There will be no more talk of dispute between us. Luke stands at my right hand and will always do so. The city is well guarded. If I should die in next summer's battles, or any summer after that, Luke will see to things until a son of mine is old enough to wear a sword."

There was something strange; not in his words but in the manner of speaking them. It was proper for a warrior to face death with a light heart, but the exultation in his voice meant more than that. Others, too, had sensed it. I saw Blaine lean forward, watching, hand tugging at his beard.

My brother said: "So one more thing: one more toast to drink! And for this we will all stand because we toast one who is not here—not in this room and not yet in this world."

He lifted the golden pot that stood between us.

"My Lady is with child. Drink to my son to be—your future Prince!"

tHREE

THE PRINCE'S LAdy

Next morning I sat with Ezzard in his parlor. Not many people were received there but it was still furnished with the trappings of a Seer. Chairs, stools and table, sideboard and bookcase were of dark fumed oak, and the long curtains at the windows were black velvet. From facing walls a stuffed owl, wings lifted, stared with small glass eyes of frozen fury at a stuffed eagle. There were three skulls on the sideboard and a Book of the Spirits thickly bound in white calf. In the center of the table stood the sphere of milky crystal on an ebony base which Ezzard was thought to use in receiving messages from the Spirits, and from the High Seers in the Sanctuary.

The radio transmitter and receiver, through which the messages in fact were passed, was in a small room above this. Ezzard showed me the panel in the wall which, pressed at a certain point, opened a way to the stairs that led to it. I asked him:

"And such things are in all the Seers' Houses? But how can you trust the workmen not to talk?"

"When a Seer's House is built," Ezzard said, "some things are done by the dwarfs, but not all. That which is sacred to the Spirits is left to the Seer and his Acolytes, and the dwarfs accept this. To serve this Order, Luke, requires more than an ability to read books and wear a solemn face and seem to pray: much more. Even the solemnity and the praying are probably less easy than you think, but there are also skills to learn and hard labor in applying them."

I nodded. "I see that."

He smiled. "You would never have made an Acolyte, but that is not your part in our business."

"Do I still have a part? After last night surely your plans for me are finished."

"Because a woman is with child? It will not even be born till summer."

"Already it makes the future."

"And may be a girl."

"The odds are against it. My father's family ran to sons, and my brother's wife was a girl with four brothers, with uncles but no aunts. And even if this one should be a girl there will be others. They will have sons, and I am pledged to aid and serve them."

"A forced oath," Ezzard said, "is not binding. It happened once before in this city, in very ancient days, that a Prince was crowned in breach of such an oath, sworn on holy relics."

I shook my head. "I want no precedents for treachery. I swore the oath and will keep it. My honor requires that. There would be no joy in living if I broke it."

Ezzard stared at me a moment in silence, blue eyes cold in the craggy white face. He said:

"What joy do you think there is in my life, Luke? Do you think I delight in this blackness that surrounds me? Not just the blackness of furnishings and clothes. My whole life is a cheat, and must be. Every day must be given up to deception, to further lies. What if my honor were to make demands? The cause we serve is greater than small things like one man's honor."

I said stubbornly: "I am sorry, sir, but it is something I cannot accept. My mind is different from yours, perhaps. I will serve your ends as far as I can, but my honor comes first."

"Yes." He paused. "Yes. And you serve us best by being what you are. I know you, Luke, and know what may be asked of you. It is a great deal. But I also know what may not be asked, and will not ask it. As to present circumstances, we will not worry too much yet."

He drew breath deeply: a sigh, if one could imagine such a thing from so austere a man.

"We must all be patient. And you and I, Luke, must not see too much of each other. It is known that the Seers protected you, but as was said last night the time for that is past. Men respect the Seers, as is necessary, but are also wary of them. The smell of this black cloth must not cling to you, now that you are back in the palace and a Captain of the Prince's army. So do not come here again unless I summon you."

"I shall still see Martin. He is my friend."

"Yes. That is reasonable. But of him too you will see less. As I have said, an Acolyte has other things to do than study and pray. He will not have much time to spare for idling in that cell beneath the Ruins."

"He told you of it?"

"No," Ezzard said. "He did not need to. We have kept close watch on you, Luke. And must do so. You are the piece on which our hopes are pinned. Nothing has changed there."

The peddler was a man in his early thirties, of medium build and height. Physically there was nothing unusual to him: he had black hair and beard, keen eyes, the stance of someone who spends much time trudging poor roads. But his clothes were not such as peddlers commonly wore. They were gayer in color and unfamiliar in fashion. Beneath a red cloak, unusually short but having a part, secured with pearly buttons, that could be let down, he wore baggy trousers of a brighter green than I could recall seeing in a cloth, and leather gaiters above his boots. These last were shiny black with silver buckles at the front.

He presented himself to Peter at an assembly of the Captains. He bowed deeply, putting one hand behind him into the small of his back, a gesture so comic that many smiled, and introduced himself in a barbarous accent. His name, he said, was Yews, and he came from the city of Klan Gothlen, in the land of the Wilsh. He offered the Prince a gift for his Lady.

It was a contraption in the shape of a small broken hoop, covered with bright stones. It was to be worn across the top of the head, he explained, and demonstrated this by opening it out and ludicrously pressing it in place for a moment over his own black thatch.

My brother thanked him gravely. He asked him how he had made his way so far, through such hazards. And how had he managed to cross the Burning Lands?

There had been a party of them, the peddler explained. For a long time his people had traded into the countries of the savages. There were risks—he shrugged expressively—but there were also profits. And for years it had been known that the Burning Lands were cooling: there were fewer mountains that spurted fire and the fires themselves, with their flows of molten rock, were smaller. There was a pass and others before had ventured part way in but had been forced to turn back—as his companions this time had also done. He had pushed on, gambling that he would get through before the heat from the ground overcame him. It had been a near thing but he had succeeded.

Peter said, looking at the polish and the shining buckles: "Your boots have stood it well. You must have good leather in the land of the Wilsh."

The peddler shook his head. "I threw away the ones I wore. They were well-nigh scorched through."

"And your horse? Did you have spare hoofs for him?"

"No, sire. But I made him boots of leather; and bound them round, as I did my own, with a cloth that we have in my country. It is woven from a stone called chrysotile which protects against heat."

A cloth woven from stone? But the very improbability made his tale convincing. My brother put other questions to him, which he answered as readily. His city lay in mountainous country and lacked the richness of land we took for granted. Their sheep gave poorer wool and stringier mutton; what corn they had was scant and small-eared. But their craftsmen, he thought, made things which our people might enjoy. He would hope to return another time and bring others.

"Your story is an interesting one," Peter said. "If we send an embassy to your city, will it be received in peace?"

"How not?" the peddler said. "In peace and with rejoicing. We are a civilized people."

Peter dismissed the peddler, with a present of gold that brought a gleam to his eye. He dismissed the Captains also, but asked me to stay. We went together to the little room where my father had liked to sit, away from the noise and ceremony of the court. He sat in my father's old armchair and turned the ornament the peddler had given him in his hands.

"Copper," he said, "though more highly burnished than is common with us. And the stones are pretty but not precious. Some are glass."

I said: "One does not expect a rich gift from a peddler. You were more than generous in return."

"There was more to it," Peter said, "than the return of a gift." He looked at the metal hoop and smiled. "For my Lady, indeed! Can you imagine Ann with such a thing? She will wear no ornaments, though I should have delight in giving them to her. I wish she would. I used to love looking at your mother in all her finery: a bird of bright plumage. I often think of her."

I was surprised by what he said, but even more by the

easy way he said it. The bird of bright plumage had died in
fire, after all, and his mother, my Aunt Mary, had paid for
it with her own life in the square outside the palace in
which we sat. This had been the root of the bitterness between us.

He dropped the hoop on a table and looked at me.

"I am glad to have you back, Luke."

He had said it before; but there was a different sound to
it here in this room with its memories. Margry, the court
painter, was dead of a flux, but on the wall opposite hung
his finest picture, of my mother sitting in a shaft of sunlight, with puppies at her feet and flowers behind her head.
I knew his words to be sincere and with that knew the
suspicions I had had—that the scene at the banquet had
been designed to trick me—were unfounded, fancies of my
own jealous nature. I realized also that he felt no guilt over
taking the place which I had looked to have. In earlier
days, although the elder, he had accepted inferior rank
without complaint. Then, as it must have seemed to him,
fate had redressed the balance, restoring the natural order.
It was for me to accept this in my turn. The pledges at the
banquet had been meant as public affirmations of the re-
newal of a brotherly bond: no more than that.

"I am well served by my Captains," Peter said, "and more
fortunate in my Lady than I could ever have hoped to be.
But I missed you. There were three Perrys in this city; then
suddenly one. It is good there are two again."

He went on to talk of a number of things, in much the
way my father used to do, and I was flattered by the confidence he showed in me. The plans of Ezzard and the High
Seers seemed remote and unreal. What did their cold

science matter compared with this? I was glad I had warned Ezzard that I would take no part in intrigues against my brother. In other ways I would help them as duty required, so far as it lay within my power, but they must accept him as Prince as I did.

The suggestion of sending an embassy to the city from which the peddler had come had not been an idle remark, it seemed, but something closely pondered. Peter discussed the form it should take: a troop of horse, under a Captain. Not a large troop, but picked soldiers who would do us credit in the eyes of foreigners. And which Captain? We discussed their merits. Nicoll or Greene, he thought. I gave my preference to the latter as less impressive physically— Nicoll was a huge, handsome man—but of better judgment. Peter nodded.

"That is right enough. And although courage and strength are enough in a soldier, it is judgment that a Captain needs most. I will send Greene."

"Can I go with him? I would like to cross the Burning Lands and see this city of theirs in the north."

He put his hand on my shoulder, smiling, and this time I was glad of its weight.

"Lose you again so soon? No. There will be other expeditions, I have no doubt. For the present, I cannot spare you."

Rudi said: "Health, Captain." He called to one of his apprentices: "Take the Captain's topcoat. And bring us pots of ale."

The Armorer's forge had not changed and nor, so far as I could judge, had Rudi himself, the Master Armorer. His arms were as brawny, his hair and beard as white. His head, it was true, now reached below my shoulder, but that was because I had grown. The pewter pots of hot spiced ale were brought by the dwarf apprentice; as usual Rudi offered me his own seat, carved with the likenesses of past Armorers, and as usual I refused it. We sat together in the warmth of the central fire from which flames leaped toward the high roof. Rudi raised his pot.

"To your return, Captain! And to your new rank." He smiled. "It seems so short a time since you sat there bemoaning your ill fortune in not being chosen as a Young Captain for the Contest. And now you are Captain in fact, serving your brother, the Prince."

"Are you making the swords yet for this year's contest?"

"Not yet." He nodded toward the sword that hung from my belt. "And I see I do not need to forge one for the new Captain, since he is already provided."

"The High Seers . . ."

"I have heard of it," Rudi said. "A Sword of the Spirits. May I look at it, Captain, or is it too holy to be touched by ordinary mortals?"

He was joking, as we both knew. He had never spoken disrespectfully of the Seers or the Spirits but like most dwarfs I do not think he took them seriously. Dwarfs were interested in real things: in goods and victuals and their own craftsmanship. The Spirits, like the campaigns of the army, were affairs with which they did not concern themselves.

"The object of a sword," I said, "whoever makes it, is to wound or kill. So since it is meant to strike it may be touched."

I unbuckled the sword from my belt and gave it to him. Rudi drew the blade slowly from the scabbard. He held it up to the light of the fire, one hand under the hilt and the other supporting near the tip. He moved it slightly, tilting up and down, so that the edge gleamed. Then, gripping the hilt in his right hand, he plucked a hair from his beard with the left. He flicked the blade lightly upward and the hair parted.

"Are the Spirits dwarfs?" he asked.

It was not a question to which he would expect an answer. He weighed and hefted the sword, turning it this way and that. I said:

"You approve, Rudi?"

He nodded, his eyes intent. He said:

"We make as good swords here as in any city in the land, and better than in most. This is not boasting; our cousins in Romsey and Basingstoke and Alton would acknowledge it. But we make nothing like this, nor could. The temper of the steel . . . . And the working of it. I would give much to see the forge on which this blade was beaten out."

I visualized him in the laboratories and workshops of the Sanctuary. I doubted if he would be shocked and confused as I had been when I first saw them. I could imagine him putting questions to Murphy and deeply pondering the replies. There would be no opposition from the dwarfs if the Seers declared the Spirits wanted machines built again. Although lacking the imagination to seek such a thing they would accept it readily enough. But of course what dwarfs thought was unimportant.

Changing the subject, I asked him about his family. He had three sons, two fully grown and skilled metalworkers, though not in armory. The third, much younger than the others, was called Hans and I knew Rudi had hopes that he would follow him—perhaps one day be Master Armorer in his turn.

I spoke of this and Rudi shook his head.

"He does not choose it."

"I am sorry to hear that. But what would he do instead?"

There was a pause before Rudi said: "He has always been a strange one, and the strangeness has grown. Do you remember once you asked me if I would have wished to be a warrior?"

I remembered it: a cold winter's morning much like this, with the Contest only a few days off. I said:

"You reminded me that you were Master Armorer. It was a foolish question."

"Not foolish. Even a dwarf does not smile all day long or every day; and even a dwarf can have vain dreams. But it is true that in the main I am content. If you asked the question of my son, though, there would be a different answer."

"But he knows such a thing is impossible."

"True. It does not stop him watching the soldiers with an envious heart. And he will not settle to a trade."

"He may do so in time."

"I hope so. He is almost your age." He hesitated. "Captain, may I ask a favor of you?"

"Any I can grant. I cannot make a warrior of him."

"I know that. But you will ride out with the army next summer?"

"If the Spirits will."

"The army takes no polymufs with it even as servants.

But once or twice dwarfs have gone, as part of the baggage train. If this could be permitted for Hans . . ."

"You think a campaign might cool the fever in his blood?"

"It is possible. And if not, it would make him happy. Or happier, at least. He is my youngest."

"I will see to it, Rudi."

"I am grateful, Captain. I would put my thanks into the making of a sword for you, but it seems you have had the help of greater skills than mine."

"If this sword breaks I will come to you for my next."

He watched as I slid the blade back into its sheath.

"If it breaks I doubt if you will need another. But I do not think it will break."

I paid my respects to Edmund's mother, she who had been Lady to Prince Stephen, in her new house. Her elder son, Charles, had won booty from the campaign against Petersfield, and had shared with the other Captains in the ransom money paid by Romsey for its army and its dead Prince's son. These things had enabled him to take her from the tiny house in Salt Street and put her in a place more fitting to her rank.

It was still not large, smaller than my home before we moved to the palace, but she was not a woman who cared for show. She had no great wit and it was clear she had never had beauty, but her two sons and Jenny, her daughter, loved her dearly. She did not often rebuke them but when she did the rebuke was heeded. She greeted me warmly, embracing me. Jenny said:

"You must show him more respect, Mother, now that he is a Captain."

Her voice had an edge of mockery which was familiar to me and could still unsettle me. She was a little less thin in the face, I thought, a little more womanly in figure. She was more than a year my senior. I said, trying to match her banter:

"It is not she but you who should show respect."

She dropped a curtsy to me. "I beg your pardon, sire. And if you could find time to school me in manners, I would promise to pay close attention."

"Leave him alone, Jenny," her mother said. "He is not back two seconds before you are provoking him again. And last summer when he was not here we had mopings and gloom and constant wonderings about where Luke was, and was all well with him."

To my surprise she blushed while making her outraged denials. I was as embarrassed, if not more so, and hastened to find a different topic. I talked of the peddler, as the whole city was doing, and of the supposed wonders of Klan Gothlen in the land of the Wilsh. It was public news now that Peter was sending an embassy there and had hired the peddler to go with them and be their guide and herald.

Edmund's mother said: "I suppose there is a reason for it, but I cannot see what. Our own land and city are good enough, I would think, without going to look for others. But men are restless creatures."

Jenny said: "I would go. Gladly!"

"Go where?" her mother asked.

"To the peddler's city, if I could."

"It is a day of wonders," I said. "A dwarf who would be a warrior, and a girl who wants to go hunting for strange cities."

"And Luke," she said, "who never changes—being neither dwarf nor girl but a Captain of the army. Being strong and brave and wise and without the tiniest bit of imagination. Lucky Luke."

We sat, Peter and I, with Ann in her parlor. This was not the room my mother had used but another. It had much less of ornament and frippery and the pictures on the walls were all to do with her religion. One showed this god of theirs, a thin, melancholy man with a golden saucer behind his head, blessing his followers; while in another his body hung twisted on a wooden cross. They were a gloomy lot altogether, these Christians, and I thought it strange that Ann herself should be so warm a person.

We talked like any family group of family matters. Peter spoke of the child that was to be born. He was full of plans for him—he was certain it would be a boy—and talked almost as though he were already with us. Ann and he wrangled, though gently, about his rearing. To Peter, of course, it was necessary, indeed inevitable, that he should be trained as a warrior. Ann did not quite oppose this—how could she?—but made it plain that she would have her say in all things she thought important: which comprehended much.

I wondered what he would be like, this unborn nephew of mine. Divided between his father's demands of strictness, the iron rule a Prince must impose upon his son, and his mother's loving gentleness, would he grow into a weak vacillating man, feeble and indulgent and vicious like James of Romsey? But perhaps—and I thought it more likely—it would be their strengths, united in their love for each other, which would mold him, not their weaknesses: so making him a warrior strong yet noble-hearted, a worthy Prince to succeed a Prince.

Ann looked at the clock on the wall, dangling heavy weights, its massive wooden carapace carved with a representation of a boar hunt in which the boar at bay had tiny gleaming tusks of ivory. She said:

"I must leave you. My bath will be prepared."

Peter said, teasing her: "I have never known such a one for baths. Every day and sometimes twice a day."

"It is a weakness," she said. "I could do without fine clothes, rich food, the trappings of the court, if you were to discard me, but I should miss my baths. I confess my sin of indulgence to the priest, but I cannot break myself of it."

"Go quickly, then," Peter said. "Take this bath, that may be your last if I decide in the morning to put you away, and take a new wife who does not make such demands on the palace stoves."

They smiled and kissed and she left us. He and I talked, as easily but on different matters. There was the question of how the troop would get through the pass across the Burning Lands. The peddler had this cloth which protected against the heat; but there was not enough for one other man and a horse, let alone a score. I had talked about it with Edmund and Martin, and Martin had suggested something. The dwarfs could make boots for the horses, as the peddler had done, and in place of the magic cloth contrive a means of trickling water down over them from a skin fixed on the saddle bow. This would serve to keep them cool.

"Your friend Martin has a good head," Peter said. "He is wasted as an Acolyte. But I suppose he would not anyway have been a warrior."

"He will fight when there is need. He fought for me in the Contest."

"And was soon down."

"Not until the second round. He brought his man down in the first."

Peter grinned. "You are loyal to your followers and I am glad of it. Let us talk of the campaign next summer. I would like you to tell me what you think of a scheme I have in mind . . . ."

I do not know how long we talked. It was Peter who broke off. He said:

"She soaks more each day. She will turn into a water nymph or give me a son with webbed feet." He made a quick gesture of contrition to the Spirits, repudiating his levity and warding off the evil thought. "We will send a maid to hurry her."

He reached for the bell rope and pulled it.

It was Janet who attended his call, she who wore her dress very high at the neck to cover the marks the Spirits had left on her polymuf body. My mother had been bullied by her servants and my Aunt Mary had bullied hers. Ann asked little and in a quiet voice, but they did her bidding almost before she could speak the request.

Janet nodded and went. When she returned a few minutes later and stood in the doorway, Peter was talking of maneuvers. Without looking up, he said:

"Well, did you tell her we were waiting? It is almost time for supper."

He had not, as I had, seen Janet's face, stricken and bloodless. She said:

"Sire . . . ."

It was her voice, broken and failing, which made him turn to her and then, running forward, catch her by the shoulders. I saw his fingers tighten and her face twist with pain.

"What is it?" he demanded. "Tell me, girl!"

She dropped her head. The words were very faint, but one heard them.

"She is dead, sire."

four

Riding North

Kermit said: "She drowned, sire. That is all."

He was palace surgeon, and had held this office as far back as the reign of Prince Egbert, Stephen's father. He was tall and thin with a face like an egg, having a fuzz of white whiskers at the bottom of the oval and a thinner matching fuzz at the top. He had two younger surgeons to assist him and treated them with contempt. His pronouncements were usually brief and always final.

My brother said: "But *how* drowned?"

"She was in her bath, and alone. She fainted, one must suppose, and slipped beneath the water."

"She was young, healthy. Why should she faint? Can you be certain she was not poisoned with some drug?"

"She drowned," Kermit repeated. "If she had felt illness,

a pain, she had a maid within call, in the next room. She could have been at her side in a moment."

Peter said bitterly: "She should have been with her, not in another room."

"That is so," Kermit said, "but it was not permitted. It is known your Lady had strange scruples."

He was speaking of that extreme modesty of the body which all the Christians had. The women wore long enveloping gowns. Ann had refused to have maids attend her in her dressing even.

Peter groaned, his whole body shaking. "If I had known . . . !"

Kermit said: "You asked, why should she faint? When a woman is with child she may have spells of dizziness. If she lies long in hot water it may be more likely."

Peter stared at him, hot eyed. "Why did you not prevent her, knowing that?"

"Prevent? I advised against too much bathing. You have heard me. She did not listen."

"You did not tell me there was danger to her."

Kermit shrugged. "There is always danger in ignoring a surgeon's words. But no harm would have come had she kept her maid beside her."

Peter was silent. He looked as though he fought against something in himself: an impulse, perhaps, to strike down this creaking old man who showed more pride than pity. Kermit asked at last:

"Is there anything further I can do, sire?"

"Can you bring her back to life?" Kermit looked at him but did not answer. "Then go!"

He went stiffly, his dignity ruffled by the brusqueness of

the dismissal. Peter and I were left alone. He shook his head from side to side and his face was creased with naked pain. He said:

"Luke, how did it happen?"

"I do not like the man," I said, "but it must have been as he says."

"If someone came in . . . and found her there defenseless. An assassin could have held her head beneath the water—so easy a thing."

"Came in from where?" I asked. "Beneath the window there is a drop of fifty feet, and a guard patrolling at the bottom. The maid was in the next room and beyond that there is the corridor and another guard. There is no way for a man to come in. And if he got in, how could he get out again?"

"The maid might have been bribed. I could have her put to torture."

"You could," I said. "But the maid was Gerda, who for years served your mother and tended you as a boy."

And who came to me, I could have added, when that mother lay under sentence of death, begging me to visit her so that she in turn could plead with me to intercede for her son.

Peter banged a fist against his head. "I think I am going mad. . . . To talk of torture—what would she think of it? But I am tormented with miseries and hates. I almost hate her, whom I loved and love. That she should have been so careless of herself: she had no right!"

I had a feeling he would have liked me to go to him, to embrace him. I could not do it. The news had shocked me as much as it had him, but there were differences in our minds. There were things I could not help thinking of, however hard I tried to put them away.

"I made a jest of it. They were my last words to her." He squeezed his eyes shut and tears ran from their corners. "If I could but call them back!"

She was buried with Christian rites. There were murmurings about this, though not in Peter's presence. At her funeral there was no Seer, no Acolytes, no solemn procession to the Seance Hall with the casket in a carriage drawn by black horses, purple garlanded, and everyone, nobility and commoners, dwarfs and polymufs, following on foot to do her reverence. Instead her coffin was taken on a simple cart, drawn by one old piebald horse, to the North Gate, and so out to the patch of ground where the Christians buried their dead. The Christians went with her, and Peter and I, but he would have no others. The ground was hard with frost: they had been forced to use low braziers to thaw it, inch by inch, so that they could dig. We stood by the grave and the priest spoke the ceremonial. A sharp wind blew along the foot of the walls, lifting a fine powder of snow, and they listened with chattering teeth. Few of them, since they were all so poor, had cloaks that would keep out the cold. Standing there, chill myself in my Captain's topcoat, I heard but did not heed. I was full of thoughts which turned round and round in my head, dizzy and frightening.

This was the second time within a few years that the Prince's Lady had died in winter, and although this time there was no ugliness of murder the gloom that settled on the palace and city was scarcely less deep. Unlike my father my brother, at the outset, looked for my company. He would spend hours talking to me of Ann, repeating over and over small things, anecdotes from the life they had shared. But whereas it had hurt me that my father withdrew into a private sorrow, strangely I did not welcome this talk, and found myself slow and awkward in response.

Sometimes the Christian priest was with us. He was a weak-looking man, small in stature and with a stoop that at times gave him a look of one of those polymufs who carry a second back upon the first. As though in copy of the Seers his head was shaved, apart from a thin circle of hair round the base of his skull, and he wore black like the Seers also but in a garment more resembling a woman's.

His voice, though, was strong if his body was weak. He talked in deep tones and was never lost for words. He was always on about this god of theirs, and there were some tales that even I found worth listening to. It seems that when soldiers were sent to arrest him, one of his men very rightly drew his sword and sliced an ear off one of the guards. But the man-god rebuked his follower, saying: "All they that take the sword shall perish with the sword." What I could not understand was what was wrong with a sword death. Was it not a better end than dying starving in a ditch, as many of these Christians looked like doing? I thought of asking the priest that, but then thought it would only bring on another flood of words and did not.

He consoled Peter, as Ezzard had done my father, by declaring that he and Ann would meet in a better world than this. Ezzard had been able to further the deception with the machine through which my mother's living voice had been captured on a moving tape, to be heard again in the darkness of the Seance Hall. The priest had no such aid, but he did well enough with words.

And I, for my part, sickened of them, and of the black atmosphere which I could do nothing to lift and which roused troubling feelings in me: even a sense, although I knew it was absurd, of guilt. I withdrew more and more from my brother's presence and he, listening to the priest, seemed not to mind. The winter wore on, with blizzards and biting cold that froze the snow in the streets into ridges which the polymufs could not shift. It seemed that it would last forever, continuing day after bitter day.

Then in a night the weather changed. I awoke to rain drumming against my window. It fell all morning, carried on a wind from the west that seemed almost warm after the northeasterlies we had endured, and long after it had stopped water dripped from the eaves as the last of the icicles melted.

Within days the trees were budding. The small green spears had a look of impatience to them, of bursting out from restraint. I felt the same urge to be free of things that bound me. I found Peter alone, without the priest, and said:

"We must talk about the summer's campaign."

He shook his head. "There will be none."

"Why?"

"She hated war, as you know."

"She was a Christian. You are not."

"But I will not lead out the army in the year in which she died. Next year, perhaps."

I saw he would not budge. But it was unendurable to contemplate a summer penned in the city with this grieving man. I had hoped the fighting would work a change in both of us. If it was not to be I must find some other way. I said:

"The embassy still goes north, across the Burning Lands?"

He said indifferently: "I suppose so."

"I asked you once before for permission to go with it. I make the same request now."

"You are anxious to leave me, Luke."

"I must do something!"

He did not respond immediately. I thought he was going to refuse and prepared to argue for it. But he said:

"If you are so eager for it, then go."

"May Edmund go with me?"

I did not need to add, if he wishes. I knew what his feelings would be. My brother turned away to the window. It was raining once more, a gray rain thick with ash from the Burning Lands. He said:

"Take whom you like. See Greene about it."

Dwarftown lay across the river, toward Eastgate. None of the houses there were tall but they were solidly built and brightly painted, and decorated with much gleaming brass. Nearly all had window boxes and when I arrived, on a Sunday morning, I found Rudi attending to his. He was putting out hyacinths which he had grown indoors during the winter. They were in full bloom—blue and pink and white.

He greeted me and took me indoors. The rooms were low of ceiling and I had to watch for my head. There were a number of cabinets and sideboards bedecked with china and brass ornaments, many warm-colored cushions lying about, and the walls themselves were painted in differing hues. In the room to which I was taken two of red faced two of yellow, and the ceiling beams were a deep blue.

Rudi showed me to a chair which I guessed was kept for human visitors: it stood higher from the ground than the rest and was generally bigger. Very much bigger—I felt lost in it. I told him I had come to see his son, Hans, and he sent a polymuf maid to call him. Although not high the houses were extensive and I knew Rudi's rambled back over a considerable area. It was several minutes before the son came.

Like Rudi he was tall for a dwarf. Had he been born of human parents a tolerant Seer might have passed him at the Showing. He bowed gravely to me and stood watching in silence from just inside the door. I am dark of complexion and hair but he was far more so, a swarthy lad with a curly beard springing. His face was broad but the eyes did not have the relaxed, even sleepy look one expected of his kind; they were alert and watchful.

I said: "Hans, your father has told me that you would like to go on campaign with the army. As a servant, of course, with the baggage train."

"Yes, Captain."

"I promised I would arrange this." The eyes watched me, showing nothing. "But there will be no campaign this summer because my brother mourns his Lady."

The eyes shivered briefly with disappointment; then he was impassive. He said:

"I understand, Captain."

His voice was low and harsh but sure. I liked it, and the look of him altogether. It was some time since I had seen him bringing his father's dinner to the forge, the pot wrapped round with towels to keep in the heat. I had paid him no more attention than any other dwarf boy; but I remembered him now and felt he had improved greatly. I had come here with my mind undecided, chiefly inclined to give him this word and go. But I said:

"There will be no campaign. But I myself will ride north, with the troop that is to go across the Burning Lands to the city from which the peddler came. I am not in command but as a Captain I may take a groom with me. I make no promises—we may not get through the pass—but if you wish I will take you."

He did not reply immediately and I thought: I have been mistaken, the notion scares him. Then he quickly crossed the room and dropped on one knee before me. Eyes staring up, he said:

"I thank you for this honor, Captain. I promise I will serve you faithfully in every way, for as long as I live and you have need of me."

It was the ritual speech required from polymufs when they came into adult servitude but said, unlike theirs, with passion and also pride. I took his hand and raised him. Over his shoulder I said to Rudi:

"Does this content you?"

He smiled. "It contents me, Captain."

I said: "He is to be my groom and we go into unknown lands with many hazards. It would be well for him to take a sword."

Hans stared at me, his chin thrust forward, a small incredulous smile on his lips. Rudi said:

"I will make it for him."

There had been no banquets since Ann's death but the Captains were called to the palace the night before the embassy was to leave. There was meat in plenty and much ale was drunk but the jests were few and there would plainly be no singing. When my brother stood up, they watched in silence.

He gave a toast to the expedition's success. Then he said, dry-voiced:

"I have another thing to say. I will not speak of my loss but you know that it was double. The last time you were assembled here you drank to my son, the Prince to be. There are Spirits, it is said, that watch for pride in men, to punish it, and maybe they sought me out."

He stood wordless for so long that the Captains grew restless. I wondered if he had forgotten what he meant to say and if I should pluck his sleeve to remind him to sit down. But he spoke at last.

"I will take no other wife and therefore will have no son. So my brother is my heir. It is I this time who name him Prince in Waiting, not the Spirits. I bid you drink to that."

When we were alone I said: "There was no need of it."

"Need enough. It is wise to say these things plainly."

"And too early to talk of having no second wife. Your mind is still unsettled by grief."

"I think not. Luke, your time may come sooner than you guess."

I looked at him. He was thinner but otherwise well enough. And I could not believe he would seek to take his life: the time when it might have happened was surely past. He said:

"If I should become a Christian I must give up the sword, and no Prince can rule without it."

"You would not do that!"

"I do not know." He shook his head. "Maybe it would please her spirit."

Martin came to me in the palace that night. To bid good-by, I thought, but there was more to it: he brought a message from Ezzard. I listened and said:

"The answer is the same as before. I am determined to go."

He said earnestly: "It is different now that you have been named Prince in Waiting again. And there are rumors . . . ."

"I can guess what they are. So people listen to the gossip of Christians now? But maybe the Christians boast too soon. Sorrow mends, and his mind will mend with it."

"Ezzard knows more of these things. And you know what rests on your success."

I had assumed he had been told enough to understand the true significance of the Seers and Sanctuary, but we had never discussed it. We had older bonds and I preferred them to this. I said:

"There are limits to Ezzard's wisdom. Has he asked himself what the Captains would think of someone who proposed himself for such a thing, and then withdrew? I think they would sooner have a swordless Prince than a coward."

"It need not seem like that. Illness could prevent your going."

"And what name will Kermit give the illness: heartsickness?"

"It would be a true fever. Kermit and his assistants have been deceived before."

That was so; it had been an appearance of illness, contrived by Ezzard in one of the four named as Young Captains, that had given me my chance in the Contest. From which so much had come. I said:

"I will have no more to do with Ezzard's tricks than is necessary. And I will go with the others tomorrow. Tell Ezzard not to try to stop me."

Martin shook his head. "He will not do that." He paused. "I envy you and Edmund."

I put my hand on his black-clothed arm and squeezed it. "I wish we could have you with us. But it would look strange, an Acolyte riding with a troop of horse. And Ezzard has need of you here, I imagine."

"You are not the only one who tires of Ezzard's needs."

He had always been frail of body compared with me. He had grown taller and matched me in height but seemed to have put on scarcely any weight. His chest was narrow, his brown eyes very big in a face peaked and white and given to frowning. It was to be expected from sitting indoors all day, hunched over books. I said:

"You could come with us. If you put off that black dress and leave the Seers."

"How is it possible? I am bound by vows."

"From which Ezzard can dispense you."

"But would not."

"If I demand it, he must. I share the secrets of the craft, remember. He will release you to me."

For a moment he looked half hopeful, then shook his head.

"It is not possible, Luke."

I shrugged. "It is true there is little time before tomorrow. And tongues might wag. But we will talk of it again when I return."

He said, speaking more to himself than to me: "It was knowledge I sought. Knowledge which is clean and pure, far above the cheating and deceiving in which most men spend their lives."

"And do you not find it," I asked, "this knowledge which you prize?"

"In part," he said. "I find others things, too. Things I do not desire but must accept. There is still cheating and deceiving."

I nodded. "And I am not surprised that you tire of it. I would not care to spend so much time playing tricks in the dark on sweating commoners. But you cannot be kept to it."

"I am bound."

The frown was more a look of pain. I pressed his arm again.

"Bonds can be loosened. When I come back."

We rode north in good weather with fitful sunshine breaking through the clouds. We were twenty-three in number: Greene with his groom, a Sergeant called Bristow, sixteen troopers, Edmund, Hans and myself. And the peddler. He had exchanged his pack horse for one of my brother's chargers. He called this a favor, praising the mount he had left behind, but I guessed he reckoned to do well out of the trade. I had looked at his old horse and not thought much of it; and he had already admitted that the land of the Wilsh could not match ours in beasts.

The thaw had continued. Snow still lay in a few sheltered patches but for the most part the grass was fast growing and hawthorn bushes beginning to be green. In places shepherds had brought out their flocks. A boy near the limit of Winchester territory left his sheep on the hillside and raced down to stand on a piece of broken stone wall and watch our passing. He stared after us for a long time; until the curve of the hill came between us. I guessed he would go back to his beasts with a heart heavy with longing, and my own felt lighter for the assurance that we were on our way—that strange and wonderful things lay ahead, and gloom and sorrow and misery fell farther behind with every step our horses trod.

It was some fifty miles from Winchester to the edge of the Burning Lands as a bird flies. But our way, of course, was less direct and Greene was in no hurry. He was a tall man, alert in bearing, given to noisy mirth in drink but with a cool mind in action. He put wax on his mustache and had a trick of rolling the ends into small tight spears. As he said, we should need their best from our horses later so there was no sense in flogging them at the start. And they had been in the city stables all winter and needed to get used to the fields.

We spent the first night in Andover lands, at a village where they looked at us with fear and suspicion until

Greene produced silver for our lodging. After that they swarmed about us and poured ale. We took a pot each for politeness' sake but though they pressed us would have no more. We were on service and under discipline, as Greene told them. Though even the heavy ale-drinkers among the men found this small hardship: the ale was thin, ill-tasting stuff. The food was not much better and the straw thick with fleas. We woke before first light, the men scratching and cursing.

From there we rode across the hills and came down in the afternoon to Marlborough, which lies as Salisbury does in a valley, but a deeper one. The town stood under Oxford sovereignty but was so far distant—more than thirty miles of hilly country—that it could almost be said to be independent. They acknowledged Oxford's Prince but their own Captain General lived in princely style and they paid only a token tax.

They struck me as dour, unfriendly people. The commoners watched our passage through their streets in silence, whereas in Winchester the sight of any troop of horse would have raised a cheer. The soldiers were as sullen and Stokes, the Captain General, was a glowering, taciturn man. He listened with evident disapproval to Greene's account of our mission. Even if the thing were possible, which he doubted, he saw no sense in it.

That night when they feasted us they unbent somewhat, but not much. Their eyes watched us and each other. I thought I understood them better then, because though the Great Hall was hung with lamps they were scarcely wanted: so bright was the glow that came in at the windows. The hills rose above the town and above the hills the sky was red, a heavy crimson from which now and then spouted gouts of orange flame. Seeing this I realized that darkness, which they never truly knew, could be a comforting and friendly thing. They lived their lives under this ominous light and it was small wonder they were soured by it. And there were ugly sounds as well—distant foreboding rumblings as the earth growled in pain.

North of Marlborough there were no roads and the going was hard. We were climbing, too, at times so steeply that we had to dismount and lead our horses. We reached a crest at last and saw what lay before us.

The volcanoes spanned the horizon in a jagged line from the northeast to the southwest. Some burned and some lay quiet. Before and between them was a landscape of desolation and horror, where rivers of smoking liquid rock crawled through a wilderness of black and gray in which was no living thing. Merely looking at it was enough to cast the spirit down.

The peddler reined his horse between Greene's and mine. He pointed west of north.

"Those peaks are dead and have been for years. The pass lies between them."

"How far?" Greene asked.

"Two miles, say, to the place where the pass begins."

"And the pass itself—another three?"

"About that."

"With a mile in which the ground is hot."

The peddler shook his head. "It is hot all the way. Or warm at least. But for a mile it smokes and you cannot put your hand to it."

Greene patted the water skin on his saddle bow.

"We must hope these things work. It will do us little good to get through with crippled horses. But delay serves no purpose." He rose, turning in the saddle. "You have been sniveling for warmth all winter. Forward now, and get your bellies full!"

We kept well clear of the smoking rivers. The shoes of our horses struck sparks from hard black rock. They had been heavily shod before we left the city but would not want much traveling on a surface like this to have fresh need of a farrier. In places there were pools of water and these too steamed. One of them, away to our right, spouted high with a noise like a thousand kettles screaming together. Although up to now there had been talking and joking among the men, they rode here in silence.

The pass, rising between two black cones, looked an easy one, though as naked and dark and arid as everything else. We stopped and fitted the leather boots over the legs of the horses. This had been practiced and they endured it patiently. The boots had been cunningly made by the dwarfs, with grease inside to ease their friction, but they must hamper the animals. Small pipes led from the water-skins to the top of each boot, from where containing rings of perforated metal would allow the water to trickle down. All this had been carefully designed, but of course no one had used it yet to ride over smoldering earth.

We led the horses first, this being our best way of judging the heat. The surface was at times hard rock, at others loose and powdery. Reaching down one could feel the warmth. The dust was like sand but large-granuled and black.

Gradually we began to feel it with our feet as well; no more than a glow under the sole at first but the glow increased and became discomfort. I put my fingers to the heel of my boot and quickly drew them back. Greene said:

"I think this is where we make our dash. Mount and release the tap on the waterskin. Stay in single file and keep a distance to avoid fouling the man in front. Do not fall too far behind him, either! Delay adds delay, and Sergeant Bristow brings up the rear. He will not be pleased if he is kept waiting."

Greene led, followed by his groom and the peddler. Edmund and I came next; then the men and last the Sergeant. Greene signaled an order to trot, then canter, finally gallop. Some of the horses whinnied—from nervousness, I hoped, rather than discomfort. My own, a bay called Garance, was quiet except for the snorting of her breath and the dull thudding of her hooves.

The ground was loose and became looser. It smoked only in patches but the patches were more and more frequent. Drops of water, flung from the horses' legs, steamed as they touched the black sand. Above on either side loomed the harsh black peaks from which this stone vomit had poured —and might again, since volcanoes could wake suddenly after long years of sleeping.

I felt Garance stumble and recover. If a horse were to fall there would be a turmoil which might be disastrous for all behind, since the track here was too narrow for one to pass another. She had lost ground and I spurred her to make it up. Not that she required much spurring; I guessed she was feeling the heat by now.

It was a long mile. The pass was unvarying and seemed

endless. The tiny trickles of water would surely do little against this vast oven we must gallop over. I tried to shut my mind to such thoughts, concentrating on my own mount and that one in front. I got too near and sand, thrown up by the horse's legs, weirdly cased in leather, stung my face.

Then from ahead Greene's voice called "Halt!" I pulled Garance in near him; the pass was wider and we could assemble. The ground no longer smoked; at least not here though higher up one saw white plumes lifting. Greene dismounted, knelt and pressed a hand into the dust. Straightening himself he said to the peddler:

"It does not get hot again, lower down?" The peddler shook his head. Greene spoke to us all: "Then get these things off before we cripple the beasts. We are through."

Only then did I look ahead and see that the pass ran downhill to a desert plain like the one we had left behind. But beyond the plain there was a forest, the trees stark yet but with branches budding green.

five

Beyond the Burning Lands

It was in a mood of relief and relaxation that we headed north. We rode in a chatter of voices that measured the tenseness there had been before. We reached a river and forded its shallow, tepid waters. Halfway across one of the horses put a foot in a hole, stumbled and fell. This was greeted with a roar of laughter, all the louder as the rider picked himself up, cursing and dripping, and berated his mount's stupidity. We knew what such a mishap could have meant at the top of the pass and so were glad to see it now. Even the one who had fallen laughed with us in the end.

The desert gave way to a scattering of sickly bushes and shrubs, to thicker undergrowth and at last to the forest edge. The trees looked normal enough at first sight though much twisted in shape; but that might have been due to the blistering breath of wind blowing down from the hot slopes so little distant.

It was necessary to ride through untracked woodland before reaching the route the peddler knew. But it was not so dense as to present any great difficulty and in places opened out into glades bearing only plants and low bushes. These were further advanced in growth than similar ones in the south, and I wondered if the underground fires which fueled the Burning Lands might lie nearer to the surface on this side, tempering the winter for them. I asked the peddler and he agreed to could be so: even much farther north, he said, there were warm pools and springs which bubbled, steaming, out of the earth.

Our talk was interrupted by a cry from one of the men. He had sighted what we soon saw was a wild boar, half grown. Greene called us to the hunt and we pursued it through brush as it ran for cover. It would be good to have a supper of roast pork instead of the salt meat we carried in our pouches but I was not optimistic of our catching the beast, especially lacking hounds.

But it moved more slowly than one would have expected and the ground stayed fairly clear. We ran it down within five minutes, Greene himself leaning from his saddle to drive his sword point in behind its shoulder. The boar died with a single ear-wrenching squeal, and the rest of us rode up to the spot.

The peddler had fallen well behind and we had time to look at the body before he reached us and dismounted. Peering between Bristow and one of the men, he said:

"Well done, Captain! That one looks as though he will provide good eating."

"Good eating!" Greene echoed in disgust. "Are you blind, man?"

"Blind? I see a fat young porker."

"Look at the tusks. And those legs!"

The legs showed why he had been easy to run down. The rear ones were all right but those at the front were short and twisted. I had thought there was something funny in his gait; he had scampered more than run. The tusks were doubled, a second set growing behind the first.

"Do you eat tusks?" the peddler asked. "It is true there is not much meat on the forelegs but he has plenty elsewhere."

Greene stared at him incredulously. "It is a polybeast. Can there be doubt of that?"

"Well?"

"And you would *eat* it?"

"Why not?" the peddler asked. "Ah, I recall—your Seers forbid it. But you will find no Seer this side of the Burning Lands."

Greene prodded the boar's flank with his boot.

"There is no need of a Seer to tell what makes the gorge rise. I would as soon eat carrion."

"Captain," the peddler said, "you are in lands where you will find many strange things. And I think if you stay so delicate you may go hungry."

"Do you say all beasts are like this?"

"Not all; but many, perhaps most, are marked in one way or another."

I could see how it would be so. In our lands, under the command of the Seers, polybeasts were rooted out wherever they were found. Here, lacking such culling, the broods had proliferated and grown wilder. The only check was nature's own. I doubted if this one would have grown to maturity, with such legs.

A silence had followed the peddler's words. He broke it himself, saying:

"And is it not also a rule that the beast be buried? Will you use your swords for spades?"

Greene brushed the spears of his mustache with his finger ends, as though reassuring himself they had not grown double or turned to horns. He said:

"Buried or burned. Sergeant, have the men cut brush to make a pyre."

While this was done the peddler watched, shaking his head from time to time. I heard him mutter: "They will learn. . . ."

The pyre was completed and, the carcass having been hauled onto it, fired. We resumed our journey. The smell of roasting meat followed us and I saw the peddler sniffing the air regretfully.

As the day waned Greene looked for shelter. The land was still wooded and we had to detour round the denser patches. Many of the trees were such as would have been uprooted and destroyed at home but Greene did not suggest we should attempt so impossible a task. I saw one whose leaves were not green but a coppery red; yet otherwise it seemed an ordinary beech.

Edmund said: "Those oaks . . ."

"What of them?"

They looked normal to me, though very old. He said:

"The other trees are haphazard but the intervals between

the oaks are regular, as though they had been planted."

I saw it was true. Once one had the knack of picking them out it could be seen that they formed two lines between which, by accident, we rode. The avenue led up the slope of a hill. Greene reined his horse, and said:

"Over there."

We saw where he was pointing. There was scrub where the avenue of oaks ended and beyond the scrub the remains of a building, big enough to have been a palace. I said:

"It might serve for the night."

He said: "It belongs to the ancient days, I would say— before the Disaster. Much of it is in ruins."

His voice had an edge of doubt. I said:

"I do not think any Spirits will have lingered there all this time." I looked at the sky where clouds which had been gathering all day were still more ominous. "And even if the roof only partly holds we may be glad of the shelter."

Greene looked as though my words pleased him. I had a sudden feeling that where matters were uncertain he might seek reassurance, and take it even from one as young and inexperienced as I. The confidence of his outward show did not go very deep. I put the thought away, as something for Peter to know. He would not have given him command of this mission had he known it before.

We rode up to the house. It was very large, almost as big as the palace in Winchester. It was built of gray stone which had weathered but kept its structure; though one end had fallen, most of the rest was intact. A terrace in front had a double flight of broad steps. We tethered our horses below, leaving a guard, and walked up.

There was a doorway, twice a man's height and of breadth to match. The door itself lay where it had fallen; it was of good wood and well carved. In the hall we surprised wild fowl which fled with screeches and flapping wings. There were signs that larger animals had been there but we saw none. Furniture which carried the stamp of skilled craftsmen was warped and rotted by weather, gnawed by rodents. On the walls hung paintings in ornate frames, some unrecognizable but others showing figures of men and women in strange dress.

We walked through rooms which were large and high-ceilinged. All were far advanced in decay. In one, tapestries were hung from the wall though several had fallen or been dragged down. These also were most finely worked. The majority were too dilapidated and faded to tell what they had shown but on one which had escaped the worst there was a battle scene. Edmund and I stared at it. He said:

"So the ancients did not do all their fighting with machines. These have swords not unlike our own."

"And armor. But heavier than I would care to fight in. Look at that helmet and the breastplate! It would surely take a farm horse to bear it, not a charger. And if you fell you would have your head sliced off while you were thinking how to rise."

Edmund looked about him. "This has been a fine place in its time. A Prince must have lived here."

He, unlike I, had been born to the magnificence of a palace. What he said was true.

"But how?" he asked. "There is no city near, not even a village. Where did his warriors live?"

"Perhaps he had none."

"Then how defend himself?"

"By the Spirits, maybe."

Edmund looked at me. He said with a note of scorn:

"Maybe. They abandoned him in the end, it seems, but after all, that is their way."

Greene and Bristow were giving orders for the night. Hans was already seeking a place for me to sleep. I saw him dragging away one of the fallen tapestries to provide me with a bed, and hoped it was less damp than some I had seen. But the suspicion was unworthy. I knew already that I had never had a servant as intelligent or as careful of my wishes.

I said: "Since we have nothing to do we may as well explore upstairs."

The staircase like the floor of the hall was marble. A crack had opened between two steps but otherwise, apart from dirt which had blown in and here and there sprouted blades of grass, it seemed undamaged, though many of the wooden balusters had broken or fallen away. Halfway up it turned on itself and split, forming a double flight to the next floor. We reached a broad wooden landing with many doors. Some had fallen and others hung from broken hinges; some were closed.

There were fewer signs of damage by animals—only small rodents would have been likely to climb the stairs—but much of decay from weather. In the first two rooms we looked at, the ceilings had fallen in heaps of cracked and moldering plaster, covering floor and furniture. In one there was a gaping hole through which one saw another room above, and past that a patch of shattered roof. We turned to others which were in less ruinous condition.

Light was draining out of the sky as the day drew to a close. The wind blew in through naked frames and tugged at a loose strip of paper on the wall. Soon—next year if not this—it would have ripped it free. I pulled at it myself and tore it off; then felt regret. There had been splendor here. The elements were doing their work of destruction in their own good time and needed no help.

Edmund called: "Luke!"

He had opened one of the closed doors and was standing just inside. It was a room which had been more protected than most. The ceiling was almost intact and both windows had glass in them.

It was also smaller and perhaps this had contributed to its preservation. There was dust everywhere but the furniture seemed unharmed and the thick red carpet, except where the moths had taken their meals, was dry and unfaded. Along one wall was a sofa, its covering also moth-scarred but otherwise intact, and several chairs were dotted about. Edmund, gingerly at first, sat in one which had a hooped back supported on wooden struts. I said: "This looks more comfortable," and headed for one with a high back and sides. It was turned the other way. I pulled it toward me—and stopped in shock.

That which sat in the chair collapsed at my jerk and in a moment was no more than a jumble of bones inside a crumpled heap of cloth, but for one brief instant I had seen it as it had rested for countless years: the upright skeleton with its grinning skull staring out of the window at what had once perhaps been lawn not forest.

Edmund and I looked down in silence. He said:

"Do you think the Disaster killed him?"

"Maybe. But it is more likely he died later. This place was strongly built but the shock that brought down the other part would surely have tumbled him from his chair. Perhaps he lived here afterward, waiting for people to come. Perhaps for years."

A low table by the chair had an intricately engraved jar of crystal glass, which was empty. Beside it lay an oblong box made of gold. I lifted a lid and found inside small cylinders of a fragile white material packed with dried grass. Or so it seemed, but the smell was not a grass smell; it had a peculiar aromatic richness.

"And this," Edmund said.

It stood in a corner and I had not seen it because of the shadows there. It was a cabinet of polished wood with a row of metal knobs near the top, containing a square glass screen with darker glass behind it. I knew what it was from a picture I had seen in the Sanctuary: the device by which our ancestors had received moving pictures through the air, across the breadth of the planet and even from the distant Moon. I stared at it in fascination. Under one knob it said BRIGHTNESS, under another CONTRAST. Words which once had meaning. Edmund said:

"A machine."

"Yes."

"But you show no horror of it."

I said quickly: "I did not realize what it was."

I turned away from the television set. Edmund said:

"You are different since coming back from the Sanctuary. As Martin is since he turned Acolyte."

I felt the sting of rebuke. We had been the closest of friends and yet I must keep so much from him. Reading my face, he said:

"It does not matter, Luke."

And I knew that was true. The rebuke was my own, to myself. I would have been jealous if I had thought Edmund put something else before our friendship, but he was not. His smile showed it.

There was a noise on the landing and the peddler came in. He poked about among the contents of the room. Neither the broken skeleton nor the television set got more than cursory glances, but his eyes fastened on the gold box.

"Genuine," he said, "and heavy!"

He moved to put it in his jacket. I said:

"Leave it."

His gaze met mine, sharp and calculating. "We'll split two ways." He glanced at Edmund. "Three. But let me do the selling. I have contacts."

"Put it back," I said.

"But why? That is stupidity. Who owns it?"

I dropped my hand onto my sword hilt. The peddler put down the box, shrugged and went away. We heard him stamp off down the corridor. Edmund said:

"He will slip up here afterward and get it. Or mark the place down for his next trip south."

"Very likely."

There would always be greed and meanness and spoiling, and maybe all good things must fall to them in the end; but at least one did not have to take part in it or watch it. In the darkness that was fast deepening, I peered at a picture in a gold frame on the wall. It was small and murky and showed an old and ugly man, but there was something about it, about the patient eyes in the wrinkled face, that caught the heart with its beauty. I read the artist's name on the brass plate underneath. Even I, knowing little of the craft, could tell that he had been a far greater painter than Margry, this Rembrandt.

When we left I carefully closed the door behind us.

Our journey continued through several days. We did not find as good a shelter for the night again, but made do. The beasts we saw for the most part kept their distance. Once the peddler took us to a village where he was known and where we could buy food. They accepted our money though the head of the Prince of Winchester on the coins could have meant nothing to them; but silver can always be melted down. The peddler haggled with them on our behalf. They sold us bread and beef, the latter in joints. I wondered what the animals had looked like on the hoof— what sort of hoofs they had, in fact, if they had any—but held my peace, and if Greene had scruples he kept them to himself. After all, who could tell what sort of corn the bread was made from?

The villagers were a rough and dirty lot, poorly fed and clothed in skins. Not all had this protection. I saw an almost naked child, shivering, blue with cold, and gave him a woolen from my pack. Within five minutes one of the men was wearing it. I would have taken it from him and restored it to the child, but Edmund restrained me. The moment we left the child would lose it again. I was not convinced, and he said:

"And be beaten for it, into the bargain. This way he may

gain something—a crust of bread thrown to him, maybe, for conscience's sake."

"Conscience? In such a one as that?"

"Who knows? And the beating would be well-nigh certain. Have sense, Luke."

These people were of all kinds—human and polymuf with a few dwarfs—and it was shocking to find that they seemed to make no distinctions: one of the leaders of the tribe had a purple mark covering half his face. But of course they were savages and could not be expected to follow civilized practices. They invited us to stay there that night and I was glad that Greene refused, even though in the end we slept under bushes and awoke in the small hours with rain soaking us.

Five days after crossing the Burning Lands we were attacked.

We had left the river valley we had followed so long and were heading, west of north, through hilly country. The track passed through a defile which narrowed toward its end. At that point our ears were assailed by a dreadful caterwauling and savages dropped down on us from an overhanging ledge of rock.

They had the advantage of surprise and one of the first half dozen dragged a soldier from his horse before he realized what was happening. They also had superiority in numbers—at least three to one though it was impossible to make anything but a rough guess. But their preponderance ended there. I saw one jump at me and slashed with my sword so that he fell howling. Another, who had first dropped to the ground, came at me from the side and hung gibbering on my horse's saddle for a moment or two before I chopped him away. Garance reared, and her descending hoof cracked the skull of a third.

The engagement, if one could give it such a name, lasted a very short time—no more than minutes. As soon as they realized we had their measure they fled. Those who had dropped on us ran off down the ravine and the rest, after yowling at us briefly, melted away also, though they were perfectly safe up there from any counterattack. They left a dozen of their fellows behind, some dead, some noisily writhing.

One reason I had felt no alarm even at the launching of the attack was that I had taken them for polymufs. They were nearly naked and I saw that their skins were not white but blue. This blue now was stained with red and examining them one saw that it was not pigmentation but paint, which covered them from their foreheads to the soles of their feet. They were true men. Any polymufs there may have been among them had either not joined the attack or had got away safely.

Their armament was pitiful, consisting of small daggers, the largest less than a foot long. One of our soldiers had been wounded, but although his arm had bled freely the cut was a surface one only. They had not even hamstrung any of the horses which had probably been the greatest risk we ran. I think the horses had frightened them as much as we had.

The peddler made more of all this than was reasonable. I heard later that during the skirmish he had buried his head in his hands against his horse's neck and might have been our other casualty had the soldiers near him not dealt briskly with his assailants. Now he hymned our bravery and discipline in extravagant terms; one would think our few minutes of parrying and beating off these decorated dervishes was a feat to be compared to the storming of the walls of Petersfield in the teeth of deadly cannon fire. I reminded myself that he had probably never seen warriors in action before but I still found his enthusiasm surprising.

We left the dead and wounded where they lay, presuming that when we had gone their comrades would return and dispose of or aid them as they thought best. Edmund had ridden ahead with Greene and Hans took his place at my side. The dwarf was happy as I had never before seen him, his face glowing. He held his sword up over the pommel of the horse. Blood dripped down the blade and stained the hilt. I said:

"There is a rag in my pouch if you wish to clean it."

Hans shook his head. "No, Captain." He gazed at the sword a moment longer and then resheathed it. "I will leave it as it is."

In the middle of the next day we reached a village standing on the confluence of two eastward-flowing rivers. The people here were not savages but wore linen clothes, exotic in style and color like the peddler's. He was known to them and they crowded round us in curiosity and welcome. They fed us well and would take no payment. We were ambassadors to the King and must be given due hospitality.

In fact, as the peddler told us, we were less than ten miles from the city. We set out to cover the last stretch in the early afternoon, resisting the efforts of the villagers to ply us with more cakes and with sweet sticky drinks that even when measured in tiny pots two inches high made one's head spin a little.

We rode up a valley between hills that drew in on either side and were backed by high mountains. The road ran close by the river and was in good condition, and we saw farms and houses, the latter so painted as to look like the dwellings of dwarfs; but the peddler, when I asked him this, said no—the Wilsh loved color and used as much of it as they could.

And gradually the houses were more numerous and packed closer together. I was riding in the van with Greene, the peddler between us. I saw what was plainly a forge, its fire visible through the open door.

I said: "That is strange, Yews, surely—a forge outside the city?"

He shook his head. "Not outside, Captain. We are in the city now."

Greene, as astonished as I was, asked: "But where are your walls?"

"There are none." The peddler smiled. "We have no need of walls."

six

KING CYMRU'S DAUGHTER

Road and valley turned a corner and there was no more doubt that we had entered a city: on either side rose buildings, high built and crowding together up the slopes. They were altogether different from those to which we were accustomed. Apart from their tallness, which could have arisen from the narrowness of the valley and consequent scarcity of land, they formed a coruscation of color, a wild profusion of towers and domes and spires. Their tops looked like spears, thrust up to the sky in bright defiance of its lowering grayness. All was sharp and pointed: the slim square towers had spikes at their corners and the domes were tined like so many gaudy onions.

And suddenly our presence was known and welcomed; everywhere faces looked down from windows or slim balconies and there was cheering and the waving of gay cloths. The pigeons must have been sent from the village to give word of our coming. This was made fully evident when, clattering along a road built of smoothly joined blocks of granite, we found the way blocked by other horsemen. Greene signaled us to walk our horses, and I saw his hand go from the gesture to touch his sword hilt. As mine, for reassurance, had already done. Not that we would have much chance against armed warriors in their own city.

But these offered us no defiance. Their snorting horses formed two lines, on either side of the road, with a single rider between. One was aware of his magnificence first. I thought he must be a polymuf giant, so tall he was, until I realized that much of his height came from the helmet which rose high above his head and ended in an even higher plume of white feathers that swayed and jiggled with each movement of his horse. Nor was that all. His breastplate gleamed silver against a yellow doublet with great puffy sleeves, and the red leather boots which came high up his thighs had ornamental silver trimmings down the sides and a row of big silver buttons at the top. I saw something else as we drew near but could scarcely believe it. The boots ended in false points, fully nine inches long, which were silver tipped. How in the name of the Great, I thought, could a man mount wearing such monstrosities; and what would happen should he need to dismount in a hurry?

The attendant warriors though not reaching his splendor were vivid enough. We would have looked shabby by comparison even on setting out, and we had traveled far and in conditions that offered small opportunity for grooming. Doubtless we were a sorry lot in their eyes. And yet . . . their boots, too, were pointed. Not quite to the length of those of the solitary rider but I would not have cared to sit a horse while wearing them.

Their leader raised one hand, open with facing palm. I noticed a broad belt and a long sword hilt, both thick with colored stones, but his aspect was peaceful. Greene signaled again, and we halted.

The man said: "Greetings. I am Kluellan, Colonel of the King's Guard. King Cymru bids you welcome to his city and his palace."

Greene made courteous reply, his mustache points bristling but his manner easy. He had a talent for such things. I watched Kluellan while formalities were exchanged. He was not a big man but small, his face dark and thin with a wispy beard. And his horse, though caparisoned with a luxury beyond anything I had seen even in Ladies' jennets, was not remarkable: I would not have exchanged any one of ours for it.

This ceremony over, the Colonel rode beside Greene at the head of our column while his horsemen flanked us. The spectators made it a festive occasion, shouting and cheering and giving vent to bursts of song in surprising unison and tunefulness. The warmth of our welcome was as much beyond normal here as it had fallen short in Marlborough. It resembled a return after a victorious campaign and looking at some of the flushed faces and hearing the wild cries I wondered if they could have been drinking. But I dismissed the notion as absurd: it was not yet mid-afternoon.

I had thought, from the gleam in the peddler's eye when my brother gave him gold and from the tawdriness of the ornament which he had himself presented as a gift for Ann, that his land might be as poor in precious metals as he had admitted it was poor in stock. His greed over the gold box had made my suspicion sharper.

It was in stupefaction therefore that I sat down that night at the King's table. The table itself, running fully seventy feet down a dining chamber half as long again, was covered by a white cloth of spotless heavy damask, so far as I could see without a join in its entire length. On it stood a variety of silver vases filled—incredibly at this season—with red and white roses. Then there were the plates. In Winchester, where we did not reckon ourselves paupers, the Prince and his companions above the salt dined off silver and the Prince himself drank from a gold pot. Here the whole table was laid with gold: plates and pots and even forks.

Later I learned there was no contradiction between this and the peddler's greed. In our cities of the south it was true, as it always must be, that some men had more than others of gold and goods. But, polymufs apart, the differ-ence between rich and poor was far less than it was among the Wilsh. The people of Klan Gothlen, all of them, loved color and sparkle, but only the nobility had possessions of much value: the commoners decked themselves with thin copper and colored glass.

The peddler, even without the gold box, had done well out of his trip; though not well enough to acquire nobility. This was something else I was to be astonished by in the Wilsh: nobility was not granted for bravery in battle but could be bought the way a man might buy a dog, or a bangle for his wife. As Yews had said, they were a trading nation. Someone like him, from being a peddler could become a merchant and, when at last able to buy a house in that part of the city surrounding the palace, be reckoned gentle for doing so.

Astonished and impressed as I was by the show of wealth, I tried to show nothing of it as I talked with King Cymru.

In person he was not unlike his Colonel, small and un-prepossessing though with quick, lively eyes and a mouth given to smiling. He was called Cymru because the Kings of the Wilsh always took that name on their accession. He was the fifth Cymru of his line.

He wore a thin circlet of gold on his head, signifying royalty, but this, compared with his other adornments, had a bare and modest look. His doublet was of green silk, its puffed shoulders and long sleeves wired with silver and its front studded with gold buttons that each carried a pearl. His trousers, of darker green brocade, ended just below the knee; beneath them he wore a woman's silken stockings and shoes of crimson leather with gold buckles.

His beard and mustache were plucked and trimmed to a neatness that reminded me of fat Jeremy of Romsey and like Jeremy, he was scented. But whereas in Jeremy this had been a thing that caused men—even his own son—to de-spise him, here, as I had already found, it was a general custom. I had caught my first whiff of perfume when the Colonel greeted us in the street, and plenty since. Per-fumers, it seemed, were important men and well paid for their services and the Perfumer Royal, a thin, white-haired fellow with surprisingly red lips, sat at this very table.

Cymru leaned toward me, his sweetness wrinkling my nostrils with faint nausea. He said:

"I am appreciative, Luke, of the honor your brother pays me by sending you, the Prince in Waiting, on this embassy. And of your own gallantry in accepting such a mission, and a journey into unknown and hostile lands."

He had learned of my rank from Greene who now, I thought, may have regretted telling him. Greene himself, though commander of the expedition, had been relegated by the King in my favor. I sat at Cymru's right hand but Greene sat well down the table.

I said: "It was not a difficult journey, sire, with no real dangers. We were well led by our commander."

Cymru smiled. "You are a modest youth."

They were serving a dish of small roasted birds. The King took half a dozen and crunched one whole. I forced myself to follow suit but almost gagged as the delicate bones splintered between my teeth. The sensation was so unpleasant I scarcely noticed what the taste was like. I washed it down but the ale seemed not just spiced but perfumed; though that could have been the King's scent lingering in my nose. Cymru was chewing with evident satisfaction and reluctantly but with determination I reached for a second bird.

He gave no sign of noticing my difficulties. Between eating he put questions to me about the lands of the south and I answered them as best I could. I was on guard, despite the friendliness of our reception, against betraying anything of importance but it seemed the King was uninterested in military matters. His questions were all about our customs, and way of life.

I myself was trying to make sense of the habits of the Wilsh. I had been shocked to see that women sat down with men at the King's table, and drank with them, and talked and laughed and jested, with no apparent regard for decorum or modesty. But my disgust at this was nothing to what I felt over something I now noticed. The roast had arrived and, accompanying it, a dish was going round full of small yellow sticks which proved to be potatoes, weirdly prepared by being sliced up and cooked in boiling fat. It went to a man a few places down and he waved it away. I saw his hand as he did so: it did not end in fingers but in two nailless digits. This was not man but polymuf!

The King saw the direction of my look but did not read its meaning. He said:

"That is Snake, my Chancellor. A capable man."

"Snake is a strange name."

Cymru shrugged. "He got it as a child—from the way he walks. His knees and thighs are jointed unlike those of ordinary men. His hands are different also."

I said, still finding it difficult to believe:

"And he is your Chancellor?"

"An excellent adviser," the King said. "I do not know how I would manage without him."

The shocks were not over for the night. After dinner we retired to another room, smaller than the banqueting hall but still big. It had several large windows, whose glass was not plain but colored and arranged to form pictures and designs. I saw birds and animals, trees and hills and rivers, and the figures of men and women. There were chairs, soft-cushioned, arranged in a crescent and I was given one at the center, beside the King. Some other nobles had seats and the rest stood behind. I saw Greene there, and also ladies standing.

Servants, who were not all polymuf, positioned themselves beneath the lamps which were suspended from the ceiling and had long chains attached to them. A sheet of white silk was let down to cover the facing wall, and the servants pulled the chains. This dimmed the lamps to no more than a faint glow. Then suddenly there was bright light on the white sheet and, a moment later, moving figures.

This did not disgust me as the sight of a polymuf at table had done, but it was unnerving. I knew what it was: a primitive form of what had been called the cinematograph, consisting of an optical system and a source of light. Our ancestors had used electricity for this last, as the High Seers did in the Sanctuary. Here a distant hissing noise told me that it came probably from the mixing of calcium carbide with water. The film was being turned by hand, as occasional jerks showed.

The plain fact was that such a thing, in civilized lands, would undoubtedly be called a machine and its use forbidden on pain of death. But here it was being operated in the royal palace for the entertainment of the King!

What was being shown was an absurdity. The figures on the screen were animals but too ridiculously drawn even to be taken for polybeast. There was a mouse and a cat, and the story told of the efforts of the cat to catch the mouse, which never quite succeeded. The cat was continually falling into traps or down holes, or being squashed by heavy things dropping on it, but none of this harmed it and it still pursued the mouse. The flickering scenes were so scratched and torn as to be barely recognizable in places, but the court seemed to watch with fascination and, though they must have seen it many times before, occasional bursts of laughter. Beside me King Cymru chuckled deep in his belly.

Edmund and I walked together in front of the palace. The terrace was more than a hundred feet long and half as broad, made of blocks of pink granite so polished and so cunningly put together as to seem a continuous stretch of stone. It was bounded by a balustrade of white marble. Behind us rose the palace, topped by its colored spires and onion-domes. In front was the river, which here broadened and tumbled down falls shaped something like a horseshoe. The palace had been built in this spot for no other reason except the view it would command. I had been told so by one of the nobles and repeated it to Edmund with contempt.

He said: "They put a high value on beauty."

"But to site a palace for such reasons!"

Edmund smiled. "Your first thought, as mine, would be that it should be a stronghold. But then you would have walls around your city."

"That also is lunacy. If their warriors were so powerful that they had no need of walls I might understand it, but when they ride in pointed boots . . . ."

"On ceremonial parade."

"Even so! And would you fear them in battle?"

"Perhaps not. But things here are not as we are used to. What enemy do they have? There is no other city to challenge them. You have seen what the outlying savages are like. A rabble."

"A rabble can turn dangerous under the prick of hunger. Or greed. This would be a fine place to plunder."

"But for the same reason is a place to fear. And the city has its defenses. It lies snug in the fold of the hills. And has its crossbowmen."

"Crossbowmen?"

"It is a sort of catapult for shooting arrows, sending them farther and faster and with more accuracy than a bowman could."

"A machine?"

Edmund shrugged. "They do not ask such questions. But the approaches to the city are lined with hidden redoubts, armed with these weapons. I think the savages would have a warm time of it."

It was the sort of thing that I should have been finding out. I said, more angry at this moment with myself than the Wilsh:

"It may be. I would still reckon that our army would cut through their defenses like a sickle through sun dried corn. All this scent and finery and women drinking with men at table. . . . Have you listened to their Captains talk? Not of weapons or horses or tactics, but of whether the new fashion of wearing belt buckles at the side will last the summer!"

"They have a still newer fashion," Edmund said, smiling. "They are much taken with Greene's mustache and have begun to wax the ends of their own. Have you not noticed? They have such a passion for pointed things I am surprised they did not think of it before. But you are too quick to condemn them, Luke."

I drew a deep breath. "At any rate it is good to be in the

open air. That chatter and those perfumes. . . . I do not think I could stand another banquet."

"Have you forgotten there is one this evening?"

"I will plead sickness."

"That would be unwise. The King's daughter is to be presented to you, remember."

I groaned. "I had forgotten."

She had been ill at our arrival with some fever that had kept her to her bed. Now she was recovered and was to join us in the evening.

Edmund looked over the balustrade at the sweep of river and the distant falls. Artificial islands had been set up in places and covered with plants that were hung with flowers. The plants were real but the flowers were made from cloth and servants rowed out each morning to see to them and change those that had grown shabby. He pointed past the islands to a building on the far bank built entirely of glass.

"Where they grow the King's roses," he said, "long before any rose should bloom. The glass increases the sun's rays and they also have braziers to give warmth. They are capable in many things."

I was not paying much attention. "Blodwen," I said. "Imagine what she will be like, with such a name. Short and fat, dark and hairy."

Edmund grinned. "Like Maud of Basingstoke, whom Jenny and I once picked for you to marry?"

A thought struck me. "If she is human at all! By the Great, she may be polymuf."

The evening usually began in the King's parlor, a large square room whose walls were painted with scenes of men and women, in scanty clothing or none, being chased by weird polymufs, creatures human above the waist but resembling goats below. Even for polymufs they seemed improbable and I asked Cymru in what part of his kingdom they were found. He told me none—they were merely fancies of the painter, based on some old legend. An unhealthy fancy, I thought but did not say, and one that I would not care to live with.

But this evening instead we met in the throne room. It was much bigger and higher, with bronze doors leading in from an antechamber and a marble staircase, twenty feet across, rising to the floor above. The walls were painted gold and the ceiling was bright blue with realistic eagles soaring in it. The throne, against one wall, would have sat three men together. It was of heavy oak, magnificent in structure and carving, but spoiled, I thought, by the usual mass of cushions. When King Cymru took his seat I thought he might sink from view in multicolored satin.

He called me to a stool close to the throne. The fancy he seemed to have taken to me showed no sign yet of waning: they probably had fashions in companions as well as clothes. I took breath before I joined him. I was growing more accustomed to the scent but was still a long way from enjoying it.

He asked me fresh questions about my city and especially about life at court. Did the Prince hunt, he asked, and if so, what? I told him boar mostly and, on his further questioning, described the chase. He said with evident surprise:

"You mean, your nobles—and your Prince—ride after them on horseback and kill them with spears? Are they so tame, then, your boar?"

"No, sire. They run well, but they also fight well when brought to bay."

"But surely this involves unnecessary danger?"

"Danger. I do not think unnecessary. There is no sport where there is no risk."

He smiled. "A quaint thought."

I had meant to tell how I myself had once lain at the mercy of a charging polyboar, and been saved from death only by my brother's alertness in my defense, but after that remark decided not to. He went on:

"We must arrange one of our hunts while you are here."

"For boar? It is not the season."

"The season?"

"At this time of year they are breeding."

"We hunt when we choose," King Cymru said. "I will have Snake see to it." There seemed to be nothing, I thought with repugnance, in which the polymuf did not take a hand. "Tell me about your brother's palace. What sort of pipes do they use to carry hot water?"

I shook my head. "We have no such things, sire."

"Then how is the palace heated in the winter months?"

"By hearth fires."

"But do they keep you warm enough?"

I thought of the Great Hall with a blizzard beating against the windows and drafts everywhere, and said with feeling:

"Not always."

"And what of your baths? How is the water provided for them?"

There was a bath in the room I had been given here, a thing like a stone coffin in which a man could lie full length. At the end it had two brass mouths and when one turned the handles above them water gushed out, hot or cold according to the mouth. It was a far cry from our tubs at home in which one must crouch with bent knees. I said:

"The servants bring water to fill them."

He smiled again, incredulously. "And you tell me that anyone born with deformity of shape must be a servant in your land?" I nodded. "Even in so small a thing as having an extra finger or toe?"

"Yes."

"So Snake would be a servant in your city, and be made to carry water for your bath?" He laughed in a high voice. "I must tell him so. He will find it very amusing. I hope to see your city one day, Luke. You have interesting customs."

His tone, ambiguous before, was unmistakably indulgent. I realized with a quick flush of anger that Cymru—this prinked and perfumed monarch—was condescending to me, was regarding us as *barbarians*. The thought was bitter. I could not get up and go— the courtesy due from me as my Prince's representative forbade it—but I resolved that I would speak to Greene and see what could be done about cutting short our stay. This King, this whole place, sickened me.

My ears had grown used to the chatter and laughter behind me in the throne room. The Wilsh were always gossiping and laughing about trifles; the din, even in so large and high a room, was enormous. Now it broke and died into a hush, and the silence seemed like a sigh. I turned my head to see the reason.

She was at the top of the marble stairs and had just started to descend. All faces were upturned to watch her.

These Wilsh were proud of their possessions and did not hesitate to boast loudly of them, but in the stillness I saw acknowledgment of their finest possession of all. There was pride and love in it.

It was easy to see why. She was utterly different from the women of the court. For one thing, where they wore gowns of clashing colors, heavy with gold embossing, and brooches and necklaces and as many as a dozen bangles on their arms, her dress was of white silk, simply cut. She had no other adornment but a necklet of gold which showed how much finer and softer was the gold of her hair. The Wilsh were a swarthy people with a few red-haired and still fewer blond. But these last, compared with her, would look dark and coarse. Her skin had a fineness, a delicacy of pink and white, such as I had never seen even in a young child. She was halfway down the stairs before my eyes could take in the details of her features. And be further dazzled: she was beautiful.

I understood why we had met in the throne room rather than the King's parlor. The staircase was a perfect setting for her entrance. It was what she would demand, from pride of beauty. I did not like her for that, but acknowledged it as just.

She came from the stairs and the crowd, still silent, parted to give her room. She reached the throne and curtsied to her father.

Then she turned to me. I smelled her scent—not cloying like the others but fresh and flowerlike. She put her hand out to me and I bent my head to kiss it, grazing its softness with my lips.

When I looked up she was smiling. She said, and even

her accent was unlike the rest, more lilting and more musical:

"I have heard much of you, Luke. I am glad to meet you at last."

I made some sort of reply, I am not sure what. Her smile held me. It was not proud after all, but warm and open. Her eyes were a deep blue, big and wide.

The chattering had started up again behind us. The Princess said:

"Come and sit by me, Luke, and tell me things."

SEVEN

The Bayemot

Only two roads led out of Klan Gothlen; that to the east along which we had come and another that ran westward up the river valley. It was this we took when the court rode out to the hunt, postponed from the previous day because of the weather. There had been a little rain and some wind and it was cold, the King said, for the time of year. This morning there was patchy sunshine and the wind was less sharp. It blew into our faces, undoing the careful set of the King's hair and beard, and jangling the bells on the reins of the jennets.

Yes, jennets. Because in the hunts of the Wilsh as in their banquets the ladies shared the pleasure of their men. This deepened my contempt for their idea of sport but offered a compensation. The King was ahead, behind his outriders, deep in conversation with his Chancellor, Snake. Ten yards behind them rode Edmund and I, and Blodwen rode between us.

It was not that I was any more at ease in her presence than I ever was with girls. I could not think of things to say and stumbled in my replies when she put questions to me. It was Edmund now who kept up conversation with her while I, for the most part, stayed silent. And yet I was entirely happy to be with her. Not just because of her beauty, though the sidelong glances I snatched dazzled me. There was something else in her—a quality that I seemed never to have encountered before, made up of warmth and liveliness and gentle goodness.

She wore a black costume as Wilsh ladies did to the Hunt—the men, even the flamboyant King, were dressed alike in scarlet jackets—but her jennet was pure white. She carried a small whip, for ornament only I guessed. These ladies did not sit astride their horses but sideways, with both stirrups against the beast's left flank. It looked a poor way of controlling even a pony, but she handled hers well. Her small hands were firm on the reins.

In my concern with watching her I did not realize she had addressed a remark to me until she reached across, laughing, and tapped my shoulder with the whip.

"Woolgathering, Luke!" I looked at her directly. "Or brooding on some great project, from the fierceness of your gaze."

"I am sorry, my Lady. What was it you said?"

She gently chided: "Not 'my Lady.' Edmund must address me so, not being of royal blood, but to you I shall be Cousin. Or Blodwen. Since you are son of a Prince and a

Prince's heir." She looked from one to the other of us. "You are very different. How did you come to be friends?"

"Through fighting," Edmund said.

Her brow creased in bewilderment. "Fighting?"

Edmund grinned. "Yes, my Lady. I insulted him and we rolled in the gutter together. And he beat me and after that we were friends. It is very simple."

"But how *could* you fight when he was your Prince's son? And how dared you insult him?"

"Our customs are different from yours. Rougher, perhaps."

"True," I put in. "But he has not told you he was a Prince's son himself."

Her eyes opened wider. "I do not understand."

"Prince of the city before my father killed him in a duel and took his place."

"Oh, no! Is that what happens in the south? Surely no one dare raise a hand against a Prince?"

"It is not usual," Edmund said, "but it happens."

"And after all this you are friends?"

"As you see."

"I see," she said, "but do not understand. It would not be so in our country. When a man makes an enemy it is forever."

And what of friendship in this country, I wondered: was that as eternal as enmity? She had spoken seriously and I realized that many complexities must lie behind the masks of smiling faces which one saw all round one in King Cymru's court. But she herself was different in this also. I was sure there was no duplicity in those bright and candid eyes.

She laughed suddenly, a lovely sound.

"But I am glad you are friends! And since your father was a Prince, Edmund, it is proper that you too should call me Cousin."

"Thank you, my Lady." She laughed again and Edmund joined in. "I beg your pardon, Cousin!"

We rode ten miles at an ambling pace to a spot where the valley widened at the junction of two rivers. There was none of the discipline of our southern hunts, and none, I thought, of the excitement either. The King from time to time called people up to ride with him, and the whole procession seemed more concerned with conversation than anything else. I already knew what great talkers the Wilsh were. Gossip which in Winchester might have passed a few idle minutes was here mulled over, sifted again and again to discover new subtleties.

At the river fork we halted. We had been followed at a discreet distance by a caravan of servants, and now they came up and erected a tent for the royal party and trestle tables on which food and drink were set out. It made a fine show. The tent was lined with blue and yellow silks and surmounted by King Cymru's pennant, showing a golden eagle with outstretched wings against a field of azure. The tables were piled with a vast weight of dainties, or what the Wilsh called dainties. I allowed Blodwen to guide me through them but jibbed at some, particularly at what were plainly, by their shells, cooked snails. Edmund had some at her persuasion; he said afterward that they tasted of nothing much but required some munching.

Later there was entertainment from musicians. They had

lutes not unlike the ones we knew but also instruments which were strange to me: some in which a stick was rubbed over strings fastened to a long curved box with a handle, and others which were blown. Their sounds were unfamiliar but sweet; and the singers, I was bound to admit, were better than ours. The Wilsh loved music, as they loved color and paintings and talking nonsense.

Then, with no hurry, the hunt was prepared. The valley was wooded, but for a stretch beside the river the land was clear of all but grass—so clear that I suspected men had done this and kept it so. From one of the carts which had followed the procession, contraptions of wood were brought and set up. They formed barriers, a little less than a man's height, covering front and sides. There were slits in them providing a field of vision and also a means of firing arrows from the crossbows which were placed two or three to a cover.

I was granted the honor of sharing the King's cover. To my astonishment rugs were laid on the ground and a soft quilted affair placed over them, to lie on while we aimed our crossbows. It seemed we must not dirty our knees by contact with the earth!

With the preliminaries completed the hunt began, though it was beyond me how such a term could be used to describe what happened. Beaters were sent into the woods, some on the far left and others on the right. Eventually, beyond our range of vision, the lines joined to form one that moved back toward us through the trees. On the way they created a great din to drive the boars out into the open space before us.

There was a shout as the first beast broke cover, followed

by several more. At my side there was the clonk of the King's weapon being fired and the hiss of arrows through the air. I had my own aimed at a point close to a patch of thorn, and saw the thorn shake and a beast crash out from it. I had it in my sights with my thumb on the trigger ready to squeeze when I noticed something else: it was a sow heavy with young.

I took my hand away and the animal rushed on. King Cymru shouted something. His own crossbow fired again and I saw it score a hit. The sow was running across our front and it took her in the flank. She crumpled and fell, gushing blood. For a moment I thought I would be sick.

Within five minutes all was over, with half a dozen beasts lying dead and perhaps as many more having made their escape, some pierced with arrows, past the covers and along the river bank. The king stood to stretch his legs and I did the same. He asked:

"Did you see the one I got?"

I nodded. "Yes, sire."

"I did not notice you fire at all, Luke."

"I was—taken by surprise."

He clapped me on the shoulder. "You look white. It requires a little time to get used to the sight of a charging boar."

Especially, I thought, when the charging boar is a gravid sow, desperately running for safety. I said, trying to make conversation that would not be offensive:

"The beaters were lucky to find so many. I suppose they must often draw blank."

"Not on my hunts!" He winked at me. "There is an earlier chase. The beasts are taken in nets and brought here.

There are delicacies that keep them from roaming for a day or two. The Master of the Hunt sees to it, but the notion was Snake's. It is well arranged, do you not think?"

"Yes," I said. "Very well."

The beaters were dragging in the carcasses, the King's kill first. The sow was not only pregnant but polybeast, with an extra rudimentary pair of legs dangling uselessly from its sides.

"A fine specimen," said King Cymru.

We moved on up the valley, heading for another thicket where we could ambush more beasts. I had a brief opportunity to speak alone to Edmund. He was as shocked as I, but warned me to be cautious.

"You show too much of your feelings, Luke. As always."

"I cannot help it."

"The King will notice."

"He has done. And thinks it due to fear."

"Do you not . . . ?"

"Let him think what he likes," I said. "He is a butcher, not a huntsman."

Blodwen rode up to us and I held my peace. The road had parted from the riverside and climbed over high ground. We reached a crest and saw a village in the dip a few hundred yards ahead.

It was very small, no more than a score of huts clustered round the road, and approaching we saw an oddness in it. Many of the huts had collapsed. An earthquake? But we would have felt it also. There was no sign of life. Then from close by a man rushed out of the cover of the trees. He was in panic fear and gabbling. What with that and his accent I did not take his meaning until others repeated the cry:

"Bayemot . . . Bayemot!"

I had heard tales of these things, which were said to live in the sea and swallow whole the boats of men foolish enough to venture out from the shore. It was also said that at times they emerged onto land, and then destroyed and devoured every living thing in their path, leaving a trail of stinking slime.

I was with the King. I said:

"It cannot be true. You have told me—there is no sea-coast within thirty miles. The man has imagined it."

"I think not," King Cymru said. "The sea is a long way off but less than a mile up the valley there is a lake. There were rumors that a Bayemot had its lair there. It seems they were true." He spoke to the man, who trembled in front of him. "Where is the beast?"

"Gone, your Majesty." His whole body shook. "It came . . . and killed . . . and went."

The King nodded. He said to Snake, who was close by:

"It will be interesting to see what a Bayemot leaves behind it. Let us go and look."

So we advanced again. A whiff of filth and corruption came from the ruined village and then the stench was all round us. The sun's rays struck through the clouds, showing more clearly the shattered cabins ahead, and I saw that they were coated with a slime which, though transparent, gleamed in the sunlight. Something wet dropped with a squelch from a jutting plank. I was glad that Blodwen and the ladies had stayed on the crest of the hill.

At close quarters both smell and sight were more hideous.

The slime was everywhere and in places frothed with a nauseous bubbling sound. Nothing moved. The villagers had presumably fled up into the woods: those that had escaped. We reined our horses, even the Wilsh nobles brought to silence.

Then someone cried: "Up there!"

I looked over the ruins to the next rise of ground, and saw the Bayemot.

Except in size it was something like the bubbles of jelly that make up frog spawn. But it was almost as high as three men, one above the other, and being flattened from a true sphere by the earth's pull was even greater in breadth. It was motionless but quivered, although the wind had dropped, and though it was nearly transparent there were darker shapes within. Were they eyes, I wondered? Was it regarding us now? Or did it move blindly, swallowing everything in its path as legend told? And the reality was more terrible than the legend. It was hard to see how anything could withstand such a monster.

It moved. With a small lurch it began to roll down the hill in our direction; slowly at first but fast gathering speed. There were cries, and with the rest I spurred my horse back up the slope. We halted on the higher ground and saw that the Bayemot too had stopped in the midst of the slimed ruins.

Snake said: "We are safe here. They travel fast downhill, as a ball does, but uphill a man, let alone a horse, can easily outdistance them."

The King said: "Look! That fool . . . ."

A man, a beater probably since he was on foot, had run up the side slope of the valley. He too was safe there if what Snake said was true, but he came down again and took the road toward us, perhaps from fear of being alone. As he moved, so did the Bayemot. Things like tentacles grew from its side, gripping the ground to pull it forward. I no longer doubted that it could see, and was seeking prey.

The man was in no danger until he fell, looking back as he ran. His foot must have gone into a pothole because he went down heavily. Someone cried: "Get up, man!" He tried and cried out in pain; he must have sprained his leg or even broken it. He made a second effort but no more. The Bayemot reached and rolled over him and his cry of fear died on that instant.

For a moment there was silence. Then I said:

"We must save him."

"No good," Snake said. "He is a dead man already."

"He moves!"

I saw, or thought I saw, an arm feebly press against the jellied horror which bore it down. Snake said:

"He has no hope."

"We cannot leave him there," I said.

"We can do nothing else," King Cymru said. "We know the courage of you southern warriors, young though you are, but that is the Bayemot. It cannot be killed."

It may be I was mistaken in finding a sneer in his tone. The Wilsh were given to banter and I was not used to their subtleties. But I had thought he read my whiteness at the sow-killing as fear, and guessed this to be sarcasm. My anger rose and would not be controlled. It was through that more than out of compassion for the man that I suddenly pressed my horse forward. There were cries but they could not stop me, and none was fool enough to follow.

Yet although I had made the move on impulse, a part of my mind worked hard and clearly. I had noticed something about the Bayemot. It resembled a frog's egg also in having a smaller black sphere within, not in the center but high up toward the top. This must surely be the brain, or what passed for brain in such a thing.

From the ground it would be unreachable. I remembered a skill we had learned when the horses were taken out into the meadows in the spring and we boys rode them without saddles. I unfastened and dropped my sword belt, freed my feet from the stirrups and pulled up my legs until I was kneeling on Garance's back. She did not jib at this but I wondered if she would face the Bayemot at close quarters. I guided her away and then, with a quick pull on the reins, back onto a course that would take her past the beast, a few feet from it.

I drew my dagger and stood up, balancing. Then I saw the full abomination of what faced me and thought I could not make the leap. The darker shapes lower down were parts of men, limbs half dissolved. I saw the roundness of a head, with hair still on it but the face melted to the whiteness of bone. Fear and nausea overcame anger and I hesitated. But pride was stronger still: I could not face a return, defeated and unscathed, to those who watched. I tensed my legs and sprang.

The very feel of it was hideous—soft and resistant at the same time, glutinously wet. It was as though my body were pressed against a giant slug. But disgust quickly gave way to pain. Where my naked flesh touched the surface of the creature it burned like liquid fire. My one reaction was to free myself. I tried to push clear; and if I had succeeded would have fled, with no more thought of pride or anger or the poor wretch whom it had been my purpose to save.

But this I could not do. The Bayemot's surface not only burned but clung. I managed to free one leg and found the other more firmly caught. It was like quicksand, but quicksand which was alive, and hungry.

My left arm was fast but the right was free and had the dagger. I looked for the small black sphere. It was deeper inside the beast than I had thought. The burning in my leg and arm spread and deepened and I wanted to cry out. But to cry would be an expense of energy, and I could spare none.

My only hope was to jab with the dagger. A single thrust might not reach the target, and if I failed that arm too would be gripped and I would be helpless. So I stabbed, hard, but instantly withdrawing. Even so it was like pulling one's hand out of a treacle jar, and treacle which stung like a thousand wasps. The flesh of the Bayemot parted but closed up as the blade came clear. But wetness had run from the wound down the monster's side, and the skin was dimpled there. I jabbed a second and third time, and went on jabbing.

The burning in my leg and arm was making me feel faint. The dimple had become a hollow but the black thing seemed as far as ever from my reach. Could it be that it was moving farther back inside the Bayemot as I stabbed? If so, I was lost: a dead man already, as Snake had said.

Darkness falling on my mind sealed off the fiery agony as well. I struggled up through it, to consciousness and the lick of flame along my flesh. It would be easy, it seemed, to drop back, let go. What did death matter if only the pain would end?

But not a death in the maw of this creature of slime and

filth! Rousing myself I knew that now I must thrust hard and deep, staking everything on one last blow. I punched my hand, with the knife clenched in it, with all my force into the hollow. The wetness yielded but also clung. I was straining to see if my blade's point had reached its target. It was not easy to make out through this viscous jelly but with a sickness of despair I thought that I had failed. The darkness was falling again and I knew I could no longer withstand it. I closed my eyes because it made no difference.

Then beneath and around me there was a vast shivering which drew me back to consciousness. Once again I thought of earthquakes and in my mind's eye saw the pinnacles and domes of Klan Gothlen falling shattered to the ground. I was glad that Blodwen was in open country. The shivering became a ripple, a throb. Whatever was happening was taking place in the heart of the monster to which I was pinned. I pulled my dagger arm and with no more than a small sucking resistance it came free. As it did everything turned liquid, a vast bubble of water which, collapsing, dragged me down with it.

I struggled to rise and my hand fastened on the half-dissolved head. But I was too far gone for nausea or even for relief. I managed to rise and totter a few yards up the hill. As I fell again I saw the horsemen coming down toward me

I awoke in my bed in the palace of King Cymru. The beds of the Wilsh were absurdly soft and they slept, the nobles anyway, in silken sheets. After the first night of tossing and turning I had got Hans to find a board for mine, to slip between frame and mattress. I realized it had been taken away and called out something about this. Footsteps crossed the room and Hans's face looked down into mine.

He asked: "How are you, Captain?"

It was only then that I felt the pain in my leg and arms. They burned as they had in the embrace of the Bayemot, though less fiercely. My mind was fogged. I asked for water and Hans brought a pitcher and gave me some, supporting me so that I could drink.

"How long . . . ?"

"Since yesterday, Captain. It is nearly midday, and time to change the dressings on your wounds."

I watched through a mist as he did this. The burns had been covered with rolled pads of linen, smeared with a yellow ointment. He removed them and cleaned my skin, which was raw and blood-red, oozing a thin ichor in places. He was very gentle, but it hurt. When I could not help wincing he drew back.

I said between my teeth: "Get on with it!"

"There is a drink they have which eases pain. They gave you some before. I will get it."

"I think it also dulls the mind. I feel as though I have cushions inside my head. Do what has to be done. And then I will have my board back before I smother in softness."

The drug was powerful. I stayed dazed until evening, swimming in and out of sleep. People came to see me: Greene, Edmund, the King himself with Snake silent and smiling in the background. I remember them being there but little else: nothing of what they said.

Blodwen came also, and her words I remember. She was not wearing white but a dress of soft brown, the color of beech leaves in winter, and her hair curled gold against it. She stood by the bed and took my hand in its clumsy encasement of linen.

She said: "You are a fool, Luke. But very brave."

I shook my head and it hurt. Although I had tried to keep my head away from the beast my skin must have grazed it. Part of my face and neck were raw, though less so than my limbs.

I said: "A fool, yes. No more."

She looked down at me, her wide blue eyes grave.

"The city buzzes with talk of you. The poets are vying as to which will be first with his epic of Luke the Bayemot Slayer, while the minstrels have already made up their songs and people gather in the streets to hear them. There is to be a banquet that will be the most magnificent in a hundred years, where my father will give you some great honor."

I groaned. "What I did was stupid and after that lucky. I want no banquets nor honors."

She smiled. "You have no choice. There are penalties to being a hero."

"I can think of one. They have taken the board from my bed and will not give it back."

"You must do as the apothecaries say. No one is free of obedience. And when you are well you must attend the banquet and accept the honor politely."

Her hand was very small against my cocooned fist. I said: "You will be there?"

She nodded. "Of course I will."

They drank my health, spilling ale on the damask cloth and clinking their gold pots. It was very noisy and through the open windows—the evening was mild and the assembly generated of itself more heat than it needed—came the distant but even heavier din from the courtyard where the whole city, it seemed, was also drinking my health in the King's ale. Then the others sat down, but the King remained standing.

He said: "There is no need to dwell on the deed which tonight we celebrate. Some of you were there, and the rest have been told of it. No man before this has killed a Bayemot. No warrior has even dared attack one except with arrows from a distance, and arrows do the beast no hurt. Yet this boy, for he is scarcely more than that, from a foreign country beyond the Burning Lands, braved the monster's grasp and had the strength and cunning to kill it.

"I have pondered how we may do him honor and it has not been easy to find an answer. Gold would be an insult, and in rank he is already son and brother to Princes, proclaimed a Prince to be. It has not been easy, but I think I have found something worthy of him and which he will not refuse. I offer him, as a gift from all the Wilsh, the greatest treasure we possess. He is worthy of it, and I think he will guard it well."

He smiled and raised his goblet, whose heavily chased gold was crusted round with pearls.

"I offer him my daughter, your Princess. Rise, and drink to the betrothal of Luke and Blodwen!"

ThE BuildiNq RATS

I do not know what was in the salve that the apothecaries put on my burns, but it was powerful stuff. The marks disappeared rapidly in the days that followed and a week after the hunt my skin showed no more than a slight redness and roughness.

Wherever I went in the city people stared at me. When I could once more sit a horse without discomfort I persuaded Edmund to ride out. We did not take either road but went north where an old track led up into the hills. The city came to an end in a huddle of workmen's cottages with neither towers nor domes, and we rode alone. The year was ripening. Trees were heavy with leaf and flowers grew out of the grass. From the thickets songbirds hurled defiance at one another in syllables of cool beauty.

There had been rain that morning and from the look of the clouds there might be more, but the air was fresh and the sky had some blue in it. I breathed it deeply and said:

"This is good. And good to be free of eyes and tongues."

"Is praise so hard to bear?"

"Maybe not when it is merited."

"You slew the Bayemot," Edmund said. "A thing unparalleled."

"And if instead the Bayemot had eaten me, what would the Wilsh have said?"

"At least that you had courage."

"Not courage—foolhardiness. And they would have been right in it. I did not save the man. I did not even attack the Bayemot to do so. I rode at it, in an ungovernable temper, because I thought the King mocked me, and jumped because my pride would not let me turn back."

We rode in silence for a while. Edmund said at last:

"They say it was small for a Bayemot. Usually they are twice that size, or bigger."

"Had it been even three inches higher from the ground I could not have reached its brain or heart or whatever it was I stabbed. As I say, folly."

"I saw you ride down at it," Edmund said. "I called but I do not think you heard me. When I saw you pinned to its side, striking at it with a dagger, I thought that I should go to help you."

"You could have done no good."

"So I told myself, and very likely it was true. I think before I act—and then think again. I am not entirely a coward, but I do not lose myself in action as you do."

I shook my head. "It was stupidity. By rights I should

be dead, and it would have been my own fault. Dead and derided by these same people who make up songs about me. The southern fool who tried to fight a dagger duel with the Bayemot. Luck made the difference between life and death, triumph and disgrace."

"And was it luck that won the Contest for you, those years ago?"

I remembered that spring day, like this one warm after early rain, and how in the last round, Edmund having three men against my two, I had ridden away unguarded and had seen him and his lieutenant come after me. And how, as they closed in from either side, I had thrown myself from my saddle and pulled him from his horse.

"When you leaped at me," Edmund said, "then, too, I paused to think. But there was no time for thinking. And when we remounted and rode at each other, just the two of us with no helpers, it was knowing I had failed before that made me fail again."

So many things stemmed from that: within days his father's death and the plunge from palace into poverty. I said:

"I planned the first part of the Contest. But in the end it was luck."

"No, I do not think you can call it luck. I know nothing of the Spirits and am not concerned with them, but I think you have a demon who serves you well. I hope he will always do so."

There was a hill with a crumbling ruin on top. It was too steep for the horses so we tied them to a thorn tree and climbed on foot. Sheep cropped the grass, bells tinkling as they moved. Many were polybeast, either in shape or color—I saw several that were not white but black. I noted this idly, not shocked as I would once have been nor horrified by the thought that they might any day be served as mutton at the King's table. "They will learn," the peddler had said, and I was learning.

The ruin was very old, in places no more than a groundwork of stone tracing a plan. There was nothing in it worth seeing. We sat on the remains of a low wall and looked down into the valley. The city was small and peaceful, no faint echo of its tumult reaching us here. Passing sunlight caught it and struck new and sharper colors from its painted spires and domes.

"A fine sight," Edmund said.

"Yes."

"When do we leave for home?"

"In a week, Greene says."

"You still allow him to think he decides such matters?"

"He was named commander by my brother."

"Tell Cymru that." He paused and repeated: "A fine sight. Do you think our Winchester would look dull and drab to someone used to this?"

He meant Blodwen, I guessed. We had not talked of the betrothal. I had been waiting for him to say something, and perhaps he had been waiting for me. This was an opportunity but the moment passed.

I got to my feet. "We had better go down again."

In all sorts of ways I was becoming accustomed to the Wilsh and this dazzling city of theirs. Their scents faded in my nostrils into a familiarity that was not unpleasant, their bright clothes and ornaments, their ways of talking and laughing and embracing each other in public—all these lost their power to shock. I grew used to the sight of Snake's misshapen hands and his weird sinuous walk, and to the other polymufs about the court. I counted ten rings on the fingers of one fat noble and the same day learned why the mouth of the Perfumer Royal was so red: he painted his lips like a woman. Both things amused me: no more than that.

The morning of the day before our departure Hans was to take our horses to be shod. I knew that whatever the qualities of the farrier I could rely on Hans himself to see it well done, but I went down there all the same. The farriery was behind the royal stables—a big place with five smiths at work. Hans was holding my horse, which had been finished. We examined her feet together and I said:

"Good enough."

Hans said: "He makes a fair job of it, for one who is not a dwarf."

The man was at work on a rear hoof of Hans's own horse. I heard the hiss of hot iron being pressed home and smelled the familiar stench of burning. It was only as the farrier straightened up that I realized that he too was polymuf, having a twisted back. He was quite young, in his thirties I judged. It had been surprising that a man should shoe horses but this was more extraordinary. As Hans had said, it was dwarf's work in our city, and jealously guarded as such.

I said: "At any rate, they should see us home."

Hans said, in a low voice that would not carry to the farrier:

"Do we return tomorrow, then, Captain?"

I looked at him. "As you know."

"There is a story in the city."

"A hundred, more likely. Which is this?"

He stared at me with heavy, dark eyes. "They say that the embassy might go back without you—that you might stay here among the Wilsh where you have won fame and the King's daughter."

I laughed. "They spin fine yarns!"

"Then it is not true, Captain?"

"No, Hans. Not true."

The last hoof was done and I offered silver to the polymuf but he refused it; all was paid by the King. I went to the stables with Hans and saw the horses put to grooming. Later we walked together up to the palace. He was never one to chatter but I thought his silence had a brooding in it. I said:

"This tale of my staying when the embassy goes back— you believed it true?"

"I did not know, Captain."

"But if it had been true—if I had chosen to stay and keep you with me, would you have been glad of it?"

He looked at me. "Very glad."

"But why?"

"Because I am a man here."

"You are still my servant, as you were in Winchester."

"And would be anywhere. It is not what I am to you but what I am to others. In this city there is no talk of dwarf and polymuf and true men. All are men."

"I doubt they would make you a warrior. There is a height mark which Cymru's soldiers must reach."

"Perhaps here I would not be plagued by idle dreams. I do not think I would."

"And your home, family—you would be willing not to see them again?"

Family ties and the love of home were deep and strong in dwarfs. They lived close with one another and were devoted to their kin. Hans did not answer at once and I said:

"Your father would miss you."

"In a way," Hans said, "and in a way be glad. My dreams remind him, I think, of dreams he had in his younger days, and put away. Of course I would miss him, too, and my brothers and sisters; above all my mother. There is always something to lose. But maybe more to gain."

He spoke with passion. I had had no idea that he felt like this. I said:

"Listen, if you would stay that can be arranged. The King will find a place for you."

"And you, Captain?"

"By the Great, Dwarf, I can do without a servant!"

I stopped, realizing what I had said. It was no insult, or I had not thought it such, and in Winchester neither of us would have noticed the term I had used. But we were not in Winchester. I said:

"I am sorry, Hans."

He smiled. "There is no need for it, Captain."

"But it is true that I can manage by myself. I am used to doing so. Stay, if it is your wish."

"It is not my wish if you are going."

"I must."

"Why, Captain?"

We had come to the gardens at the rear of the palace. There were lawns, so smooth and so finely clipped that from a distance they looked like squares and circles and crescents of green cloth. Gardeners trundled cutting devices up and down. They were on wheels, and a bladed cylinder turned with the wheels and sheared the grass. In Winchester they would have been called machines. Between ran walks of finely sifted red gravel, leading to continually splashing fountains. Wooden casks, brightly painted, contained flowering shrubs brought from the glass house across the river. Above us loomed the palace, with all its domes and towers.

I said: "To give news of the embassy to the Prince, my brother."

"Captain Greene can do that."

There were swans on the river and one of them flew low across the gardens with a heavy flap of wings. Before I could speak again, Hans went on, more rapidly.

"There would be advantages in staying, Captain. The King favors you."

"So does the Prince of Winchester."

"In Winchester there are intrigues."

I looked at him in surprise. He was dwarf to me still and the remark improper. I said with some sharpness:

"There are intrigues in every city. Here, too."

"Of a different kind. No plotting for thrones, no daggers in the night. The King is safe, and the King's friends. They intrigue for amusement. In Winchester the business is in deadly earnest."

I thought of the Blaines and the Hardings. I said:

"If you have heard of anything that threatens my brother . . ."

He shook his head. "No, Captain. But the possibilities are always there. As you know."

It might be that he referred to that intrigue which had deposed Prince Stephen and raised up my father. I looked at him closely, ready to be angry, and saw nothing in his face but concern for me. I said:

"Enough, Hans. If there is to be trouble at home, the more reason for me to return. But my offer to you stands. Stay if you wish and I will obtain the King's favor for you."

"No," Hans said. "Thank you, Captain, but I will not stay."

That which Hans had told as gossip of the city took on hard substance within minutes of my leaving him. A messenger from the King told me Cymru desired my presence. I was taken to one of the smaller state rooms and found him in talk with Snake on a matter of taxes. He did not dismiss his Chancellor but bade me sit with them.

He did not indulge in the long preliminaries which were common among the Wilsh but put the matter to me at once and plainly. There was no need for me to go south with Greene. His people did not wish to lose me. Nor did he. Nor, he added with a smile, did his daughter, the Princess.

I hesitated before replying. He must have taken this for encouragement, because he went on to say that I need not worry as to wealth or position. At the banquet, it was true, he had conferred only one thing on me, though that his most precious possession; but it carried benefits beyond itself. I would be made a Count—house and servants would be put at my disposal, and the means to maintain them as befitted a person of rank and nearness to the throne.

I shook my head and said that I had not been concerned with such things. Cymru said:

"But you hesitate?"

"If it is the King's wish that I stay, then of course I must."

"No, Luke. It is for you to decide, freely."

"Then with permission, sire, I will return with the embassy."

"You are homesick for your own land? Our ways must be strange to you, but I thought you had grown more used to them."

Snake scratched his neck with his two-pronged hand and I felt scarcely a twinge of nausea. I said:

"It is not that."

"Then?"

"My brother may have need of me."

"It is a good answer," Cymru said. "The best you could give. But you will come back to us, will you not, Bayemot Slayer?"

"Without doubt."

"Good!" He clapped my shoulder. "And we will trust our lands stay free of Bayemots till your return."

I smiled. "And after also, sire, I hope."

Blodwen said: "Luke, there is no need for you to come back here."

I looked at her, unsure and uneasy and said, knowing the words stupid as I spoke them:

"I have promised, Cousin."

Her expression was troubled, her fair brows frowning. I had seen little of her since the banquet. I thought she had been avoiding me and my feelings concerning this were mixed. There was disappointment, resentment, some relief, but much uncertainty in my mind. Now, walking down the stairs that led to the throne room, I had heard her call and stopped for her to catch up to me. We stood together halfway down, with no one in sight but three lads stripping the wall that faced the throne, and those too far away to hear our talk.

"The promise does not matter," she said.

"To me it does."

"Listen," she said. "You did a great thing, and my father likes you. He offered you something, and how could you refuse? Or not promise to return and claim the gift? But no one has to accept a thing he may not want, even though a king gives it. And no one is required to keep a promise that stems from such as this."

"I accepted the honor gladly, and promised freely. So I will keep my promise."

She gave a small sigh that had exasperation in it.

"Luke, you do not help me! What I am trying to say . . . In your country, I know, things are different. Edmund has told me that your women commonly do as they are bid, and are married as their fathers command. We of the Wilsh have more freedom. The women share in men's lives, and choose him they would take as husband. I am the King's daughter, and bound by that, but I believe, as do all girls here, that people are people, not puppets to be dangled and twitched by those who hold the strings."

I was uneasy still and puzzled. It was not the first time I had failed to follow the shifting quickness of her mind, but this was more important because she was more earnest.

I said: "Who is calling you a puppet?"

She put her beautiful head on one side and stared at me.

"I see I must speak more plainly. You said you gladly accepted an honor. But I am not an honor: I am Blodwen! And you will keep your promise to return? But I do not want you to return to claim your prize, because I am not a prize but a girl, with my own thoughts, my own feelings. I am not to be given away as a trophy even by my father. If I am not sought for myself I will not be sought at all."

I said: "Anyone who sees you must seek you for himself. It has nothing to do with Bayemots or prizes."

I spoke from the heart. She looked at me and, after a moment, nodded and slightly smiled.

"That is something, Cousin! I am not sure yet how much but it makes a start."

She had lost me again, but I felt a softening and was grateful for it. I said:

"You were going to show me your pavilion across the river. Will you let me row you there?"

She smiled more fully. "Of course, Luke."

We went down the stairs together. As we reached the bottom a thought struck me.

"We have talked of what I might seek, but what of you?" She raised her brows in question. "You also had no voice in what was said that night at the banquet. And you have said you would not be a puppet. Would you prefer it if I did not come back to Klan Gothlen?"

She stopped and stood before me, her blue eyes an inch or two below the level of my own.

"I have been wondering when you would come to that! It is better late than never."

"But the answer?"

There was a space before she smiled, and said:

"What girl would not want you to come back—Luke of Winchester, Conqueror of the Bayemot?" She pointed to the three who were working. "Do you see what they are doing?"

"Stripping the wall."

"In preparation for the great painting that is to cover it. Half a dozen of our finest artists, under the guidance of the great Gwulum himself, will work on it. It is to be called 'Luke and the Bayemot,' and even with six of them it will take a full two years to complete."

She laughed and slipped her arm in mine, and I thought myself answered. As we went through the antechamber, she said:

"But I will be my own woman. Always. Remember that, Luke of Winchester."

Cymru had wanted to load us with magnificent gifts, far surpassing those we had brought him in my brother's name. We had resisted this, pointing out that we were no trading caravan but a troop of warriors, and could not travel heavily burdened. So the things he gave us were small but costly. A dagger, pretty to look at and heavily jeweled but of no practical value; a chess set with elaborately decorated pieces in gold and silver; a book telling the story of the line of Cymru, its cover pearl and ivory and its pages full of finely detailed paintings in brilliant colors—these and many more.

The royal guard which had received us provided escort for the first part of our journey. I noticed that the men wore ordinary boots, not the pointed ones with silver tips, and left their plumed helmets behind. They rode well, moreover, and with discipline. At a place where two roads crossed they halted, forming lines for us to ride between. As we did they cheered us, uttering a wild cry in the ancient language of theirs which they still kept in part. We cheered them in return, and rode on. It was wooded country and they were soon lost to view.

I was sorry to be going away from Blodwen but I traveled with a light heart. I had learned to like the Wilsh better than I had thought I would, and been amazed by the beauty of their city, but Winchester was my home. Each mile brought nearer the moment when I would see the high walls with the pennants fluttering above them, and hear my horse's hoofs clatter on the stones of the High Street as we rode up the hill toward the palace—not so splendid as King Cymru's but more dear.

During our stay in Klan Gothlen I had not seen much of Greene and his attitude toward me at first was strained and distant. I won him round by at once making it clear that, whatever the situation had been there, here I accepted him as commander of the troop with myself as his very junior lieutenant. He was amiable at heart and if there had been rancor it did not last.

We rode and bivouacked and slept, and rode again. Four days passed with little of note. Once a party of blue-painted savages, like those we had encountered on the journey north, hurled insults at us from a distant ridge; but made no attempt to come to closer quarters. From villages we bought food to supplement our rations. In one there was a breed of polyhens bigger than turkeys, some so gross that they could not walk and had to have grain brought to them to peck. Their eggs were more than four inches in length. I was amused that Greene showed no scruple about buying them, and the fowls also, for roasting that night for supper.

In the middle of the fourth day we made a halt at a village which had been deserted. There was no way of telling why because there was no sign of life or death, only rotting huts that steamed in sun following rain.

A man called Deevers, who was known as a scavenger, wandered among the huts. From behind one he called: "Captain!" and Greene and I went to see what he had found. He pointed to something which at first sight looked like a part of the back of the hut. Then I thought it was the crude construction of a child. All sorts of things had been used in the building: twigs and small branches fallen from trees but also pieces of wood and metal culled from the ruins of the village. The structure they formed was weird and seemingly without plan, though I noticed at the front a ramp leading up from the ground to a hole that gave access to the interior: a narrow ramp and a hole only a few inches across.

Deevers said: "Rats ran out, Captain." His voice held loathing. "Big ones. More than a dozen." He pointed again. "They ran into the grass there."

"The building rats," Greene said. "I have heard of them. So this is what they build."

He wasted little time in looking. His boot crashed in savagely, shattering it and scattering the bits of which it had been made. I spoke involuntarily:

"Why do that?"

"Polybeasts," Greene said. "And rats, which is worse. Even your Wilsh friends would kill them, I think."

I did not know what to say, or what I truly felt. My own horror of rats was deep, from a time when I was a child of three and a cat brought a dead rat to me as a gift and left it on my pillow while I slept. But along with this detestation was something else: a hatred of seeing any built thing, even one built by rats, so wantonly destroyed.

In the end I said nothing. Not all the rats had fled at Deevers' approach. There was one that emerged now from the rubble of its home and launched itself at this enemy giant, trying to claw and scrabble its way up Greene's boot. He knocked it aside easily and broke its back; and then ground under his heel the helpless hairless young which their mother had stayed to defend.

That night we camped near another village, this time inhabited. It clustered round a knoll that overlooked a few patchily cultivated fields and the river whose valley we were following, and we stayed on a similar small hill half a mile to the south. It had a thatch of trees on top, like our own St. Catherine's, which afforded some shelter.

I was restless and could not sleep. Maybe the incident with the building rats had disturbed me more than I had thought. Perhaps it brought to the surface of my mind the confusions which had grown during my stay in the land of the Wilsh, and the deeper confusion between my life as it was and as the Seers planned it. Things which had looked simple in the clear context of our life in the south now showed themselves to be difficult and complex. The Seers had taught me that there was more to the world than the clash of warriors and cities. But I had not realized how much more it could be.

The restlessness increased and I got up. The others around me were sleeping. A three-quarter moon sailed clear in a space between clouds. One of the two guards saw me; I spoke quietly to him and walked on. My horse whinnied, and I patted her neck.

The mounts had been tethered to outlying trees under the guard's surveillance. In the moonlight I felt his eyes on my back also and, wanting to be alone, went down the hill and out of his range of vision. Elsewhere it was a sleeping world. From the village on the other hill came neither light nor sound, not even a dog's barking.

I came to the track along which we had traveled. To the north lay Klan Gothlen; to the south, beyond the Burning Lands, my native city. Both seemed very far away, and not in distance only. In this thin, silent realm of black and silver it was hard to think of them as real.

Trees overhung the track. I heard a sound above me, very small, perhaps no more than a bird shifting on its perch. All the same I looked up. But the dark shape was already dropping onto my shoulders, and before I could cry out strong fingers clutched my throat. They pressed a point in my neck; and thought and memory ended.

NINE

THE EYRIE
of THE Sky People

I recovered my senses to a rhythmic pounding sound that I thought at first was the beat of blood in my temples. My next realization was that I could not move—and yet was moving. It took me several moments to grasp that my limbs were bound and I was being carried along at a rapid pace. The pounding was the thud of the feet of those who carried me.

My face was toward the ground and not far above it. Occasionally a tall weed whipped against me, sometimes painfully. In the moonlight I could see the dizzying rush of the earth under me and the steadily jogging feet: four pairs, naked but not flinching from the roughness of the ground. So four men had my roped figure slung between them. But there were more in the band; other feet thudded alongside these. I tried to estimate how many, but it was hopeless.

They ran in silence apart from an occasional sharp word of command; and effortlessly and with apparent tirelessness. I had no idea how far we were from the place where I had been captured, but knew I was being carried farther at a pace not much less than that of a trotting horse. I debated calling out and decided it would do no good. A nettle slashed my cheek, and I bit my lip in silence.

They ran for what seemed like hours before they rested. I was dropped to the ground, bruising my shoulder against a stone. At last I could see something other than the sickening sweep of the earth. There were perhaps twenty of them. They lay motionless, as though they too were bound, and still without talking. I heard the murmur of their breathing; that was all.

Eventually there was another barked command and the trek began again. My four carriers, or perhaps another four, picked me up as casually as I had been dumped. The ropes which bound me had four loose ends, a few feet long, and they twisted them round their shoulders with the skill of long practice. My face was upward now; either by accident or because by this time we were far enough away from the camp for it to be unimportant what landmarks I might see.

Not that I saw much more—only four straining backs and the sky above. But I was glad of the change when they forded a river. I was held scarcely above water level with the back of my head dipping in and out. As it was, I thought I would choke from the waves that splashed over me and filled my nostrils.

There was a second rest break that followed the same

routine as the first. When they started off again the paleness of dawn was challenging the moonlight in the east. I thought our progress was more upward but could not be sure. My limbs were stiff and sore from the ropes, my skin smarting from a hundred small abrasions. All I could think of was an end to this monstrous journey.

It came in a way I could not have foreseen. We were in a forest, with huge trees blotting out the growing light of day. The runners pounded along a narrow track that wound between them. From the front came the cry which had previously signaled a break. I expected to be tossed to the ground and braced myself against the shock of landing. To my astonishment I found myself being pulled upward instead. The two men holding the ropes attached to my shoulders were shinning up the opposite sides of a broad-trunked tree. They traveled with a dexterity that reminded me of squirrels. Once or twice I bumped, but fortunately the tree's surface was smooth, with no projecting branches. Above was complete blackness. I wondered how branches could be so dense or leaves so thick—with a few oddly regular holes. One grew in size and I saw we must pass through it. This happened, and there was light again. With a quick jerk my captors tossed me clear. I thought of falling the height of the tree—thirty feet at least—but I fell no more than a foot and landed softly.

They left me there. I was on a level surface through which the trunks of trees projected, giving the impression of a bizarrely dwarfed forest. This surface seemed to join them together. Huts had been built on it to form a tree-village. The softness under me came from a sort of moss, deep and springy in texture.

I could not see where the two who had carried me up the tree had gone: perhaps into a hut. I saw no one else and no one came. From the golden light breaking through the tree tops it was plain the sun had risen. I was sore and bruised and aching, the softness of the moss only making me more aware of my discomforts. All the same, and despite the growing evidence of day, at last I fell asleep.

I was awakened by being prodded in the ribs; not roughly, more by way of appraisal. I tried to jerk away but the ropes held me. I opened my eyes and saw what was happening. An enormously fat woman, in a shapeless brown dress, was nudging me with the big toe of a large and very dirty foot. When I stared she looked down at me indifferently and, after one last prod, waddled away and disappeared into one of the nearer huts.

In about ten minutes a figure appeared from the same hut. This was a man and could have been one of those who had taken me: he was sinewy and had an athlete's walk. I saw with a shiver of fear that he carried a knife, and made an effort to free myself. A futile one; I had discovered already that their skill in roping equaled their running.

He reached me, stooped, and with a quick flash of the knife cut my bonds. The ropes parted and fell away. I tried to move my arms but could not: cramp held them. The man began to rub my arms with his hands. His fingers were firm and sure, kneading the muscles into life. He said:

"What is your name, stranger?"

His accent was far more barbarous than that of the Wilsh but his tone was surprisingly friendly. I said warily:

"My name is Luke."

"I am Jan." His face cracked into a distinct smile. "Welcome, Luke, to the eyrie of the Sky People."

I asked: "Why did you bring me here?"

He went on rubbing and smiling. "The stiffness will soon go. Then we will find food for you. I am sure you must be hungry."

They were very strange, these who called themselves the Sky People. The men all showed the amiability of Jan, and were as talkative as they had been silent during the long run through the night. In the village it was the women who scarcely spoke and who ignored me, after that first prodding with the toe. They were immensely fat; even the girl children were balloon-bodied and moon-faced. They ate a great deal, being served with food before the men took any, and did no work of any kind. It was the men who swept the huts, brought fresh moss, made plates from big evergreen leaves which they stitched into the shape of dishes, and even cooked the food. This last was not done in the tree-village but somewhere on the forest floor, and brought up in wicker panniers.

It would have been impossible, in any case, for the women to climb and I realized eventually that they never, from birth to death, left the village. The men were strong and lithe and skilled hunters, bringing back beasts of the chase, and grain and dairy products which they exacted as tribute from nearby earth-dwelling tribes. These they despised, but they cosseted and seemed almost to worship their gross womenfolk. All decisions were left to them, in particular to the one I had first seen and who was their Chief. The men vied with each other in offering tidbits to the gaping maw which was her mouth. Her appetite matched her size and weight. Once a pannier of cakes was brought up and I saw her munch a good three dozen, washing them down with gargantuan drafts of ale.

The men, of course, had built both the huts and the floor of interlaced branches on which the village stood, and kept them in repair. The moss was a polyplant which grew plentifully in the forest. Apart from its softness, it was resistant to rain and protected against heat and cold. The huts were lined with it and it was also used to caulk the external cracks. It kept the huts warm in winter when the trees were leafless and gales blew in from the west and north.

They were cunning builders. In a wind the trees swayed all round and the floor creaked in a manner that alarmed me, but everything held firm. They had also, as I discovered on my first night there, built an equally strong wooden cage in which I was placed and the door padlocked. (The lock and key were among the very few metal objects they had apart from their daggers, and I do not think that they themselves worked metal at all.) I had a bed of moss which was not uncomfortable and they gave me blankets, but there seemed small chance of my getting free. The bars were of thick wood and stoutly roped together. If I could have got hold of a knife . . . but they watched me closely.

Yet in a friendly manner. When I repeated the question as to why I had been captured and brought to the village they grinned and shrugged and countered with questions of their own. There seemed little point in refusing to answer these, and they listened with great interest. They had heard of the city in the north and looked impressed when I told them I had been there, and that the King himself was my friend and had given me the signet ring I wore on my little finger.

This they examined, passing the band of gold with its blue stone carrying the eagle seal from one to another. They would take it, I thought, to give to one of their fat women, and I resigned myself to the loss. But a thought struck me. I said to Jan:

"The King has many such treasures. And others which would please you and your Ladies. Silver mirrors in which they can look at themselves, precious combs for their hair. If you send him a messenger, carrying that ring and word from me of what is needed, he will give them as ransom for my release."

They were fascinated by this notion, as I had hoped, and discussed it volubly. A ring for every woman in their tribe? I promised it on Cymru's behalf. And smaller ones for the girl children? That, too. And these mirrors and combs of which I spoke—what were they like? I described them and they hung on my words. I said at last:

"Is it a bargain?"

Jan said: "We must ask the Chief."

I knew him better than the others and had thought at first he had some position of importance. But I knew now that, when they were inside the village at any rate, all men were equal, and equally subservient to the women. I said:

"But you *will* ask her?"

"Of course! Two rings each, do you think?"

This element of bargaining raised my spirits further.

I said: "Two, assuredly. Will you ask her now?"

He looked shocked. "She is resting and must not be

disturbed. Later I will." He took the ring from a comrade and gave it back to me. Gesturing to the others to draw near, he went on: "I have made a new poem. Listen."

It was another peculiar feature of these peculiar men, who were both silent-running hunters and yapping house-wives, that they had a passion for making up verses. Jan recited while the rest listened and then noisily applauded. I knew little of poems but this one struck me as particularly bad. I thought it politic, all the same, to join in the applause.

I spoke to Jan again in the evening. He said:
"The ransom? Ah, yes. The Chief agrees."
"Then you will send a messenger to the King?"
"Of course. Hear this, Luke.

> *"Our huts are swayed*
> *By tempests from far lands,*
> *But like our hearts are anchored*
> *To our high-branched home."*

"Very good," I said. "Can I see him?"
"Who?"
"The one who is to go as messenger."
"That will be arranged. The Chief will see to it."
"But the ring?"
"I will give it to her to give to him."
"And the message?"
"Say it."
"It would be better written."

He said with scorn: "We do not write things down. We can keep them in our minds."

They did have remarkable memories. Some of their poems were extremely and regrettably long, but no one ever fumbled a word. I said:

"Very well. Say: To King Cymru, greeting from Luke of Winchester. I am well but need your help. Grant safe conduct to the bearer of this ring and message. Send him with . . ." I broke off and looked at Jan. "How many are your womenfolk?"

"More than a hundred. The Chief knows."

"Then twice that number." He looked at me inquiringly. "Two rings for each, you said." He nodded, smiling. "Send him with so many rings, and this will secure my release from captivity. I will repay the debt. Do you have that clear?"

He repeated what I had said without hesitation. I offered the ring and he took it. I said:

"The mirrors and combs . . ."

"Oh, yes."

"They would burden a running man." Jan nodded in agreement. "But you can trust me to send them afterward."

"Of course." He laughed. "We can trust you! my poem, now—should it be 'tempests,' do you think, or does 'winds' sound better? 'Winds from distant lands,' perhaps?"

I calculated that it would not take the messenger more than six days to reach Klan Gothlen. Allowing two days' sojourn and another six for the return journey made fourteen. I ticked them off in my mind. Sitting one evening just inside one of the huts, while rain dropped from the eaves and soaked away into the moss, I said to Jan:

"He will be there now."

"Who is that, Luke? And where?"

"Your messenger. He will have reached the city."

"Oh, yes." He smiled. "And then he will come back with the rings and you will leave us. But not before the Celebration of Summer, I hope."

"What is that?"

"We have two great festivals, one in the winter at the year's turn and another in summer. There is feasting and singing, and we save our best poems to say then."

I said with a brave attempt at enthusiasm: "A great festival, indeed. When does it take place?"

"In a few days." He squeezed my arm reassuringly. "I am sure you will not miss it, Luke."

Two days later there was excitement which obviously concerned something that had happened on the ground below the village because it centered on a man who emerged from one of the holes and ran to the Chief's hut. When he came out gossip buzzed round him. It was just possible, I thought, that the messenger had returned. I said so to the two who were with me and they went across to see.

Someone had come from the world outside but not the messenger. It was a peddler, with cloth to sell. The Sky People made no cloth, though the men cut and sewed garments for both themselves and the women. They bought the material from itinerant merchants, and this was such a one. The Chief had commanded that he should be brought up with his wares. I saw her waddle from her hut and sit heavily on her special seat outside. I thought, though maybe it was fanciful, that the whole floor gave a creak of protest as she did so.

At the hole men were hauling ropes. Bundles were brought up and then the peddler. An ordinary dark-bearded man in a peddler's cloak—but young, I thought, to be his own master. He was lifted clear and stood on the mossy floor. I saw with surprise that he was a dwarf. And in the next instant recognized him: It was Hans.

He did not see me for some time, though his gaze, while he spread bolts of cloth from the bundles, was covertly ranging round the village. The cage standing outside Jan's hut obviously interested him. When he did catch sight of me he merely gave a small quick shake of the head. It was unnecessary: I had no intention of revealing that we knew each other.

I wondered how he would get a message to me, but in fact he did not try. When his business was finished—they bought several lengths of cloth in dull blues and browns— the bundles were tied up again and they and Hans dropped back through the hole.

I felt a keen disapointment at his departure. Later I reflected that this must have been a scouting trip. Greene and the rest would be hiding nearby, ready to attack at the right moment.

Jan came to me, smiling. "I am glad the peddler arrived at this time. Our Ladies will have new dresses for the Celebration of Summer."

I said: "They will look beautiful in them, I am sure."

He said approvingly: "You speak fine words, Luke. You will do us much honor at the feast."

"If I am still here."

He laughed. "Of course! If you are still here."

I was wakened when my arm was touched by a hand that reached between the bars of the cage. As I jerked upright there was an urgent whisper:

"Captain! It is I. Hans."

It was very dark, the waning moon hidden by clouds. I peered and saw the blur of his figure. I said, also whispering:

"Where are the others?"

"There are none."

"But Greene, Edmund..."

"They went on, thinking you lost. Captain, I have two knives. Take one. We must cut the ropes and get you out."

He handed me a knife and we set to work. It was harder than one would have thought. The ropes were deeply embedded in the corners of the cage. It was necessary to saw awkwardly at them and the darkness did not help. Nor did the fact that the knife slipped and cut the base of my thumb. This was painful, but the greater nuisance was that my hands became slippery with blood.

There was a cough from inside Jan's hut and we hunched into immobility. When nothing more happened, Hans began hacking away again. I tried one of the bars; it seemed as firmly held as ever. I whispered:

"We are getting nowhere."

"Patience, Captain. We will in time."

"Listen," I said. "I am not sure this is necessary."

I told him, speaking softly through the bars, of the messenger who had gone to Cymru's court for ransom. He would soon be back. If we were discovered in this attempt at escape they might call off the deal. And they might kill him—their ways were not predictable.

He heard me out, and said: "There will be no ransom."

"But they have agreed it."

"They were deceiving you. I have spoken to villagers in this region. In a day or two these people hold a feast . . ."

"They have told me of it."

"But not all, I think. The women rule here. There is an ancient custom of the tribe. Twice a year they sacrifice. At one time it was a young man from among themselves. He was turned loose in the forest, hobbled so that he could not run, and the women hunted him. When they caught him he was tied to a stake and spit-roasted over a fire. Then eaten. The custom changed. The women grew too fat and idle even to hunt a shackled man. They let their men bring a victim from outside the village. So twice a year they run and make their capture. It is a point of honor to travel great distances—because of that the nearby villages do not fear them. They took you for this purpose."

I could not believe him. I thought of Jan and the others, reciting their poems to me, and looking for approval. I said:

"But they have been friendly . . ."

"A farmer is kind to his cattle if he wants them to come fat to the knife."

"But the ransom!"

"They wear no jewels or adornments. They despise them.

This is well known. It is true of their women also. I was told not to waste my time offering them brightly colored cloths."

Realizing this small truth convinced me of the larger one. I had been a fool not to see it. They had bargained with me as an amusement only, and all their seeming friendship had been a mocking lie. I remembered saying to Jan that he could trust me to make up the rest of the ransom. He had laughed as he agreed. Rage swelled in me. In that moment I would have thrown my life away just to have my hands around his throat.

Hans said: "A strand has parted. Keep on."

I turned my fury into a renewed onslaught against the ropes. I cut myself again but paid it no heed. We sawed away and gradually, strand by strand, the ropes yielded.

Hans whispered: "Now, Captain! Push, and I'll pull."

I strained against the bars. They gave slightly, and then resisted. I put all my strength into forcing them. Suddenly, with a loud cracking noise, the whole side of the cage gave way and collapsed with Hans underneath it and me on top.

As we were scrambling free there were sounds of movement from the hut. My eyes were more accustomed to the dark and I saw a figure come out and thought I recognized Jan. My anger had cooled and thoughts of escape were stronger than desire for revenge. We must get to the hole and down the tree. But he had seen what was happening. He gave a yell for help and ran, not in our direction but to the hole.

We could hear others moving, responding to the alarm. In a few moments they would be swarming round us. Even if Jan did not manage to delay us long enough for them to catch us up here, they would be down the tree and after us almost immediately. And they knew the tracks through the forest as I knew the alleyways of Winchester, and were trained and expert runners.

But slight as the chance was, we must try for it. I started to run, then realized Hans was not following. I cried: "This way! but he was bending over something: a small pack. I did not know what he was doing, except that it must be a waste of time. I went back and tried to grab his arm.

"Come on!"

He shook himself free. There was a smell of oil and he had something in his hands: a tinderbox. Flint sparked against steel and the tinder caught. He thrust a wad of oily rag at it. It flamed, and he tossed it as far as he could toward one of the huts. As it arced, burning, through the air, he lit another wad and threw it in the opposite direction. A new and different cry of alarm came from Jan and the figures that were tumbling from the huts. Fire shot up where the first missile had landed. They ran toward it, and then broke in confusion as a second fire started behind them.

Hans said: "Now, Captain!"

We ran for the hole, which was no longer guarded. I heard shouts but did not look back. Hans had climbed the tree by means of the spikes in its side which the men of the Sky People used, but he had brought a rope with him and made it fast at the top. He wanted me to descend first but obeyed when I ordered him to go. As he slid down I could take in something of the scene. The moss had caught over a wide area in both places where the burning rags had landed. Figures were dashing about and trying to douse the flames with blankets. Then Hans jerked at the rope and I took it in my hands and dropped.

Above us a red circle glowed and opened out, and was followed by another. Bits of burning moss dropped like shooting stars. In their light I could see something of the ground: the kitchens at which the men had cooked food and the spring-fed pool from which they took water. And a pit, a little longer than a man, heaped with charcoal, with blocks at either end that had rounded, lengthwise grooves in them. Grooves in which a stake might rest and be turned like a spit. Sickness and anger rose in me again. I looked up and rejoiced at the spreading fire. The cries were thinner but more anguished. I rejoiced at that, too.

Only when we were clear of the forest, whose whole heart seemed to be consumed in a conflagration that crimsoned the sky like the flaming mountains of the Burning Lands, did I remember the children trapped in it with the rest. Then I felt only sickness, and no more anger.

I pieced together from Hans the manner in which he had gone about my rescue. I was not missed from the camp until morning, the guard having changed shortly after I spoke to the one on duty. Then Greene instituted a search for me, and closely questioned the people of the village. They claimed to know nothing and when the place had been ransacked it was plain I was not there. Greene searched two more days before abandoning me as lost and taking the troop onward toward the Burning Lands.

Hans, being only a servant and a dwarf besides, could not dispute the decision, but the next night slipped away, taking gold from my pack which, together with the rest of my gear and my sword-belt, I had left behind. His only idea then was to make a search of his own, with little notion of how to set about it. But at a village he met a peddler and gave him a good price for his mule and goods and cloak. A peddler could travel anywhere and pick up news.

It was not long before he heard of the Sky People and of their twice-yearly expeditions in search of a victim. Very likely the people in the first village could have told Greene, but had not done so for fear of reprisals from one side or the other. It was safer to know nothing. Hans learned roughly where the village lay and headed for it. The nearer he came the more information he could glean. It was in a village at the edge of the forest that he learned that the Sky People did all their cooking on the ground because the moss they used dried quickly and when dry burned easily: these villagers themselves used it as tinder. In the tree-village no flame was permitted: the moss kept them warm enough even in winter to have no need of fires. Because of this he had brought the tinderbox and oily rags with him.

I said: "You saved my life, Hans."

"I am your servant, Captain."

I shook my head. "No longer. Henceforth you are a warrior."

"A dwarf."

"That makes no difference."

"It will in southern lands, in Winchester."

"Leave that to me," I said. "I will see to it."

We traveled on foot, having too little gold left to buy horses; we sold the mule also to buy food. And extra boots. Because that was the way we crossed the pass through the Burning Lands, carrying water-soaked boots, three pairs each, on strings around our necks, and putting fresh ones on as those we were wearing began to roast our feet. We ran as fast as we could over the smoking black sand, with the boots unlaced so that we spent as little time as possible changing them. I was a near thing, even so. The soles of our last pair were crisped and each step an agony by the time we could discard them and walk, limping and barefoot, down the slope into the valley of black rock.

We bought new boots not in Marlborough but at a village outside. I avoided cities and did not make myself known as we journeyed south. The pigeons would have flown with news of my return and, childishly perhaps, I wished to keep it as a surprise. Fortunately no one would take us for anything but vagrants in the ragged clothes we wore.

So at last we came into the Itchen Valley and saw St. Catherine's Hill, bushy-topped with trees, and a score of other familiar sights; and then the city itself, not towered and domed like Cymru's, but strong and lovely behind its walls. We came to the West Gate and the guard challenged us. I saw his commander on the step above him: a Captain called Barnes whom I knew well.

I cried to him: "Greetings, John!"

He stared at me.

"Do you not know me? It is Luke. Brought back from the dead by this warrior dwarf of mine!"

He took a step forward but did not speak. Had I changed so much that he could not recognize me, I wondered: not even my voice? I said:

"Will you let me pass to go to my brother?"

"I will do better than that," he said. He raised his hand. "Guard, arrest this traitor!"

TEN

The Sword
of the Spirits

When I was first taken down to the palace dungeons there was a drunken man in the next cell. In between singing and shouting insults at the jailers he demanded to know my name and the reason for my imprisonment. I did not answer him; as far as the latter was concerned I could not. To my own questions Barnes had only replied that I would be told what was necessary when it pleased the Prince to do so.

Later the drunkard was taken away, in a final flurry of oaths and objections, leaving me isolated: my cell was one of a block of four and the other three were empty. I wondered if they had done it from fear that I might use even so unlikely an instrument as that to further my supposedly treasonous activities. It was a relief to be free of the din the drunkard made but the silence that followed, broken only by a drip of water down the wall of the cell, soon became still more oppressive.

The cell was some nine feet square, stone flagged, with an iron grating and a bucket in one corner and a heap of straw in another. Chains were attached to iron stakes that were driven in between the granite blocks that made up the walls. It was some consolation that I had been left free to move about. The walls were unpromising surfaces on which to leave mesages but previous dwellers here had done their best. I read "Jesus Saves," presumably written by a Christian because that was the name of their god, and a man's name, Roger Anderson. The letters were crude but a quarter of an inch deep. It must have taken months of patient carving.

I thought how unconcernedly in the past I had heard of this or that person being sent to the dungeons. While I was jousting, or talking with Edmund and Martin, or just lying idle in the sun, Roger Anderson had been crouched in these clammy depths, scratching with a piece of metal, perhaps a nail, against hard stone. And outside at this moment the world went on—people gossiped and laughed, loved and fought—as indifferent to my fate as I had been to his.

An iron grille over the door provided light, coming in the first place from a small window, also barred, high up in the passage. It was little to start with and faded into blackness with evening. I had no way of telling time. The monotony was only broken when a jailer, carrying a lantern, brought a jug of water and half a loaf of stale bread. I asked him what o'clock it was but he did not answer. He slammed and locked the door behind him, and the flicker of light went away with his footsteps until the next door cut it off. I drank from the jug but felt no hunger. Rats got to the loaf in the night and devoured all but a crust.

My mind revolved uselessly on possibilities and reasons. It must be something to do with King Cymru, I thought, but could not imagine what. But whatever had been said of me I was confident that I only needed to see Peter to put it right. I knew I was no traitor, and could meet any man who accused me.

Time dragged by and I could not sleep. Yet after I had resigned myself to being awake all night, sleep suddenly overcame me. And when I awoke it was light enough to see my surroundings again, though dimly, and a key was grating in the lock. I struggled up from where I had been lying cramped and cold on the straw, expecting the jailer with more bread and water. It was he who opened the door, but he stood aside for another. My brother Peter looked in at me.

He said: "Well, Luke, I find you poorly housed and bedded. But at least you are back with us. I cannot tell you how bitter a disappointment it was when Greene returned and told me you were lost."

His voice was calm, even light in tone. I said:

"I would like to know of what I am accused and who accuses me. I was told some nonsense about treason."

Peter nodded, as though in approval. "I see that a night in the cell has not cooled your spirit. I am glad of that.

As to the charge . . . treason covers it but it has another name also, different but no less ugly. The charge is murder, and I accuse you."

"Murder?" If I had not been shivering so hard I think I might have laughed. "Whom have I murdered?"

"Someone who did you no harm, who loved you even. Your Prince's Lady. And with her your Prince's heir."

His voice had not changed, was steady still, but as I grew accustomed to the light I could see his face more clearly. There was a look in it, in the eyes particularly, which I had seen before. His mother, my Aunt Mary, had looked like that when she raged at me for supplanting him and afterward when she waited, in a cell much like this, for the burning to which she had been condemned.

So he was mad: he must be. The grief which Ann's death had brought had rankled and turned into this sour lunacy. I felt the chill of fear. I said:

"Will this charge be made in court?"

"It has been made, in your absence. You were found guilty and condemned. All that is necessary is the execution."

Could he have paraded his madness in open court, and nevertheless got a verdict from the Captains? One had heard tales of crazed Princes enforcing the whims of their derangement, but not in Winchester. Our Captains, surely, were made of stronger stuff. The chill deepened in my belly. I said with what calmness I could muster:

"I was with you when your Lady left us to take her bath; and with you when the maid brought news of her death. I did not part from you in the time between. So how can I be guilty of her murder?"

"You covered your tracks well." His face had a small, cold smile. "I grant that. But a murderer does not need to be present when his victim dies."

"Poison, you mean? But Kermit told you she died from drowning. Do you say he was lying?"

Peter stared at me. "You are a better fencer than I thought, but it was to be expected. Shall I tell you a story? After you had gone with Greene's embassy my restlessness grew worse. I missed your company: does it please you to be told that, you who were my brother? And the pain of losing my Lady grew worse also. I could not bear to look at that part of the palace which had been hers. So I gave orders that it should be pulled down."

He paused and I waited. If not mad then he was mistaken, and given opportunity I could prove it. I knew my own innocence.

"Massy, the Builder Dwarf, saw to the work. One of his men found a strange thing and showed it to him, and he showed it to me. A line ran under the floorboards to a small room, fifty feet away, that is used for lumber. The line was made of some black stuff but had metal wire inside. And the wire was joined to the metal foot of the bath in which she died."

Now my mind was in turmoil, half understanding, half refusing to believe what he was telling me. And yet he could not have made it up. He said:

"I called in Strohan, and asked him what he knew."

Strohan was the palace butler, in charge of polymufs but himself true man, heavy and solemn and bald of head.

"He spoke freely when he had seen the wire and where

it led. Last year his only grandchild died, a girl of six, drowned in the river below the mill. His wife went to the Seer, as women do, and got messages which he said the child had sent from the spirit world. She believed this, and believed it also when the message came that the Seer and his Acolytes needed to do secret things in the palace and to have a certain room kept for them. The poor fool thought it would help the child's ghost return to her, and Strohan did as she wished. So the work was done one day while my Lady was absent, giving thanks to her Christian God for the child she was to bear. And then they killed her, from a distance. With a machine!"

He paused, and again I said nothing. He said:

"Does this surprise you? I think not. But surely it is an incredible thing—that a Seer should use a machine to kill? I do not think the Captains would have believed it, except that when we sent men into Ezzard's house without warning we found the machine, and words written down for using it. It eats oil and spews out something called electricity which is invisible. It is a poison, it seems, that is more powerful when it works through water. That is why the wire led to the bath. The machine struck at her only for a moment and left no trace. It stunned her, her head fell under the water, and she drowned as Kermit said. The plot was cunning and cunningly carried out."

I said in a dry voice: "I knew nothing of it."

"So Ezzard said, until we showed him the machines we had found. There were many. I could not understand them all and would not wish to"—his voice cracked with disgust—"but I think it likely they have had many uses.

To make voices in the Seances, and crowns of light, perhaps, foretelling a great future for a Prince in Waiting? Ezzard took you with him to the Sanctuary, and brought you back. So you say you knew nothing of this?"

"Nothing of killing."

He said with contempt: "Lying will not save you. You are the Seers' man and have been from the beginning. They took you away when our father was murdered and I became Prince. Then, when they knew she would bear my son, they killed my Lady. All this was done for you, so that when I too had been slain you would rule in my place."

"It is not true." He looked at me and laughed. I thought of some of the thoughts that had come into my mind after Ann died, and of my hopes that he would turn Christian. "I had no part in it."

"You lie, but it does you no good. Will you beg for mercy next?"

I set my eyes to his. "No, I will not do that."

He laughed; more loudly and the madness was in it.

"Then you save a little of the breath you have left! You will need it for screaming when you and your friends hang in chains in the palace square and fires are lit under you."

"My friends?"

"I kept them for your return. When Greene came back without you I had a mind to kill him for his carelessness in losing you. After all, you were my brother and mean more to me than the others. But only you and your Seers kill the innocent, so I held my hand. Then I set a date for their execution. I chose Midsummer Day which the Seers have always called a day sacred to the Spirits. This year I will offer them a fine sacrifice. And on Midsummer Eve itself you return from beyond the Burning Lands to make the sacrifice complete! If that too was the Spirits' doing, I am grateful to them."

"Martin . . ."

"Your Acolyte friend? You will see him. I will hang him next to you as a favor."

"He had no part in any killing. I will swear to it."

"No more than you did?" The words were a sneer and I had no answer. He would not listen to anything I said. "No matter. The time is past for oaths and lies, for words of any kind. There is merely an end to bring about, and this day sees it. You are lucky to spend so short a time under sentence. It is an advantage over your friends. But I will tell the executioner to make up for it by giving you a slower death."

He stared at me, his hand on the hilt of his sword.

"I thought I might have pleasure in bringing you this news, but you fill me too much with disgust. That you should have plotted her death, who begged me to call you back from exile . . ." He shook his head. "I must not think of it or I would kill you now. And you do not deserve such mercy."

He turned and went. The jailer slammed the door and their footsteps echoed as they walked away.

The day was gray and warm, heavy with rain that had not yet fallen but seemed as though soon it must. But even if it fell in a torrent it would not quench the oil-soaked pyres of wood and straw heaped at the foot of the stakes in the palace yard. There were nine, and at eight figures hung in chains from the crosspiece: Ezzard and his Acolytes. The ninth was vacant.

A space had been cleared in front and soldiers guarded it. For the rest the square was crammed with people—the Captains and their Ladies on chairs at the front, other citizens of high rank behind them. Behind them again, the mob. They were hurling their derision against those already awaiting execution but as I was brought into the square under escort the jeers and yells rose to a higher pitch. Their faces were white foam on a shapeless sea of hatred, but as I was taken past I saw one I knew. It was old Parr who kept the sweetmeat shop in Leather Lane. My mother had given me halfpennies to buy from him when I first could walk and talk; and when I won the jeweled sword at the Contest he had stopped me in the street and rambled on interminably about old times. His face was different now: a spitting image of loathing.

I was brought to my brother where he sat in the midst of his Captains. There was an empty chair beside him, signifying his lost Lady. He said in a cold steady voice:

"Luke Perry, you stand condemned, by the people, the Captains and the Prince of this city, of murder and treason. The sentence is death by fire."

He had spoken into silence. At those words there was a cry of what sounded like protest. I learned later that it came from the Christians, who rejected such a punishment even when the victim was one of their own. But the mob drowned this small outcry in their vast roar of approval, and blocked the attempts they made to get through to the Prince.

I said: "I am not guilty of this charge."

They roared again, with anger. I saw Edmund standing behind his brother, Charles. His face was drawn and white. Even at this moment I could feel sorry for him. He had said he had wanted to aid me against the Bayemot but had not acted because he thought he could do no good. Nor could he now. It might be that he believed the indictment true.

He could not help me, nor could anyone. Ezzard and Martin hung in their chains on either side of the stake in the center which had been left for me. It was higher than the others, for the harder death which Peter had promised. I remembered Edmund's words on the hill above Klan Gothlen: "You have a demon who serves you well." Now as never before I needed him.

Peter's raised hand quelled the tumult. He said:

"The city finds you guilty. I, your Prince, confirm sentence. Executioner, see to it."

It was the formula. The executioner stepped forward to take my arm. I shook free and said in a loud voice:

"No Prince but a usurper! I was named as my father's successor."

If I had wanted to say more I could not have made myself heard for the din. If they could have got to me I think they would have torn me in pieces as hounds break up a hare. But once again they obeyed Peter's lifted hand.

He said: "The Seer named you. Ask him again, above the crackling of the flames. Maybe you will be a Prince yet, in the land of the Spirits."

They howled with mirth at that. I shouted:

"I name you coward!"

"Burn him!" Peter said. "Burn this traitor, who killed my Lady."

The executioner's grip was stronger now and one of the guards held my other arm. The crowd was yelling, but I could be heard by Peter and the Captains. I said:

"When Stephen challenged my father, after he had been acclaimed as Prince, he took that challenge and fought and killed him. But he was a true Prince."

I watched his face. There was no need to take notice of my words. A challenge from a displaced Prince was different from that of a felon, condemned for murder. No one would hold it against him if he did not accept, nor even think it ignoble. But I saw his eyes narrow and knew my shaft, however feeble, had gone home. He got to his feet.

In the new hush he said: "Maybe you think to get a quicker and easier death. Do not deceive yourself. I accept the challenge but I will not kill you. You will smolder no less for having a bloody arm. Bring him a sword!"

He looked a worthy Prince. He was several inches taller than I, broad of shoulder but narrow in waist and hips. His long fair hair was thick, his beard and yellower mustache fierce. He was dressed not in finery like King Cymru but in a Captain's leather jerkin, steel studded at the front, with a simple blue linen blouse underneath. The Prince's sword, forged by Rudi's grandfather and well tried in battle, hung from his belt.

By contrast I was a ragamuffin, my clothes tattered, boots scuffed, skin dirty from the journey and the night I had spent, unwashed, in the dungeon. I was tired, and weak with hunger. There was no sense, the jailer had said that morning, in putting even stale bread into a belly that the flames so soon would shrivel; and his wife kept hens who could make good use of it. And the sword that was given me, whether by accident or design, was more a boy's than a man's: scarcely longer than the one I had won, three long years ago, in the Contest.

We circled each other, and the iron of his boots struck sparks from the cobbles. I had hoped anger might unbalance him, but he showed no signs of it. He smiled, and said in a level voice:

"You are returned a great warrior, I am told. Greene told me of your exploits before he knew your crime. Luke, the slayer of the Bayemot, who won a king's daughter in the land of the Wilsh. . . . I am honored to face your sword."

I lunged while he was talking. He parried, back-handed, without breaking the rhythm of his speech. Steel struck steel and the shock jarred up my arm. I darted back, expecting the riposte, but he stayed where he was and laughed.

"Is this the Bayemot-killer? Is Bayemot the name the Wilsh give to rabbits?"

I thrust once more and was beaten back, and thrust again. I called in my mind to my demon to aid me, to bring me the strength and fury that I needed now as much as when I had struggled in the clinging embrace of the monster. But he would not come. Instead I saw the gentle face of Ann and my brother's mask of grief. I was innocent of her murder but she had died because of me. That much was true.

Again I came at him but my blows were like the wing beat of a fly against a hornet. The crowd cheered him on but he needed no encouragement. Once my foot slipped and, still smiling, he allowed me to recover.

He mocked me. "You sweat. Are you warm, rabbit-killer? You will be warmer soon."

Then, as I attacked, instead of passively taking the blow he struck. Fatigued and sick at heart as I was, I could not but admire the way he did it, pivoting perfectly and smashing his sword across my own. My nerve endings were shot through with pain. I staggered and fell, and the sword dropped from my numbed fingers. He took a step forward and put his boot on it.

"And now," he said, "will you walk to the stake like a man, or shall I prick you on with my sword point?"

The mob was shrieking for joy. I looked up at him, smiling with hate above me. I thought I heard my name called but it could only be in derision. Then I heard it again, through the baying.

"Luke!"

I turned my head. Edmund had pushed through beside his brother. He had something in his hand: another sword. The sword I had left in the camp when I went out to walk in the moonlight—the sword the High Seers had forged for me in the Sanctuary.

He sent it skittering across the cobbles. Peter could have struck me down as I reached for it but did not. He said:

"I think now you have run out of friends and swords. One more makes no difference."

My hand closed round the hilt. I had one friend in the

crowd, as Peter had said, and it had taken great courage to do what he had done. Courage in a cause which he must be sure in his heart was lost. And another friend, hanging in chains and waiting for the torch to be put to the straw at his feet. At last the demon rose and I leaped at my tormentor with an angry shout. They might give me whatever death they could impose, but they would not make me go tamely to it.

Peter knew the difference with a warrior's instinct. There was no more careless ease and no more mocking. He fought with skill and coolness and professional silence. The crowd, also sensing the change, quieted in their turn. I heard nothing but the thud of our feet, the clang and hammer of our swords as we traded blows. Once there was a deep indrawn sigh, from a thousand throats. It was not until blood trickled down my arm and split in heavy drops on the stones that I realized what had prompted it; and that I was hit. I had felt nothing.

Always his strength forced me back. I battered against a moving wall of steel, and muscle that seemed no less hard. I slipped a second time and he did not stand back but came after me. I twisted away from the blow which, had it landed, would have sliced my arm off at the shoulder as one carves a chicken at table; and darted clear. He moved swiftly, swinging his sword in an arc of brightness through the dull air. Then I met him, with every ounce of strength I could muster, in a downward smash that matched his own. Metal shrieked in the clash, and the agony of the shock almost made me fall. But I kept my balance and my sword. And saw his, broken to a stub only inches from the hilt, the blade shattered and useless at his feet.

For a moment we stared panting at each other. I could scarcely draw breath to speak. At last I said:

"I am innocent of her death, as Martin is. Keep your city and your title. We will go elsewhere, my friends and I."

His answer was a howl that was neither of grief nor rage. It had both in it and more: madness and despair. He rushed at me, swinging his broken sword, and could have wounded me, even killed me, had I not jumped clear. He turned and came again. I thrust for his right shoulder to disarm him. But he leaped, careless of defense, seeking only to reach my skull with his shattered weapon, and the point of my sword took him between the ribs. His weight and the impetus of his charge wrenched it from my grasp.

But he lay on the cobbles, unmoving, with the point thrusting out through his back, and his blood gushing from beneath him. The stones were not stained for long. In the silence that followed, while people strove to take in what they saw, the first thick drops of rain fell from the sky. After that it came in a torrent, washing his blood away.

My first act as Prince was to make Edmund a Captain. He sat with the others in the Great Hall when Ezzard was brought to me. I said:

"Before Prince Peter, my brother, you were charged with using machines, with treason, and with murder. Each of these crimes is punishable by death. His court condemned you. Do you have anything to say against the sentence that was passed?"

He stood there, very tall in his black robe which was torn at the sleeve and rust-smeared from the chains. The deep blue eyes stared above the beaked nose. He said:

"No, sire."

"What of your Acolytes?"

"They acted only under my orders."

"All of them?"

"Not all. There were some who knew nothing of this."

"Name them."

He spoke three names and the third was Martin's. I felt the tremor of relief run down my legs. I said:

"Do you swear it, as you stand in the shadow of your death?"

He said in a cold, bleak voice: "By the Great Spirit, I swear it."

"Then the sentence on those three is rescinded. On you and your accomplices it stands. For the crimes which you confess you must die in the palace yard. But we will have no more burning. The ax will take your life."

The tall, thin figure bowed toward me.

"I thank you for this mercy, sire."

My legs trembled still, and I shifted my feet to hide it. I said: "Take him away."

When the High Seers came I received them with formal ceremony. Later we sat in private in the little chamber behind the Room of Mirrors. Lanark said:

"You have done well, Luke."

I said: "And so have you. Ezzard is condemned by the High Seers as well as by the Prince of Winchester. You bring us a new Seer to replace one whom false Spirits drove mad. And the true Spirits speak again in the Seance Hall."

Lanark watched me. He was very old, with brown grave marks on his hands and face. He said:

"Ezzard also played his part."

"I am tired of this playing of parts," I said. "We talk of men, not actors. I saw him die. The axman, I suppose, was nervous, never having taken the head of a Seer before. It required three blows to finish him."

"At least you saved him from the fire."

"And those four others who merely did as they were told, and helped him lay the cable and set up the generator? They obeyed orders and died for it. But whose orders did Ezzard obey?"

"No one's," Lanark said. His voice was tired. "And he did not tell us what he planned to do."

"Can I believe that?"

"It is true. He did many things without consulting us. It was by his doing that your father was made Prince. He was a man of initiative but the initiative was not always well based. There was no need for this, and it put everything at risk."

"Including his life and those of his Acolytes. But if there had been need and the risk acceptable . . . you would have had her killed?"

His eyes were old, too, and weary from looking into a broken past and a golden future which would not come during his life. He said:

"We want a better world than this, Luke. Science and human knowledge are not ends in themselves. We use tricks and maneuvers, but we do not murder the innocent."

He had given me my answer and I knew he spoke the

truth. It was a good answer but all the same I felt regret. I had been ready to disown and repudiate them, to forget the dreams of a new age of peace and order, and think only of this city I had won and that other one beyond the Burning Lands. It would have been much simpler. I said:

"So it goes on."

"It must," Lanark said. "You have served us well, Luke, but more is to be done. Much more."

When they had gone I sat alone in the little room. Through the open window came the sound of the din in front of the palace: the crowd cheering and shouting my name. Less than a week ago these same shouters had jeered me as murderer and traitor and jostled each other for a better view to see me burn. Now I was their hero and their Prince, crowned that afternoon by the High Seers themselves—an honor no Prince of any city had known before. In an hour or two the Captains would drink to me at the coronation banquet. And soon I must go out onto the balcony to let my people see me.

It was triumph, I supposed, but it brought no joy. I sat in the old chair in which my father had sat, and Peter after him. On the wall hung Margry's painting of my mother. In skill it was not to be compared with those in the high-towered city of the north, nor with that small likeness of an old man in the ruined palace in the forest; but it touched my heart as those had not.

There had been so many deaths since hers. I had been a boy then, and now was Prince of Winchester. And the rain had washed the cobbles clean of my brother's blood.

The distant voices roared:

"Luke! Luke!"

I knew I must go and show myself to them. And after that there were things to be done: the high and necessary duties of a Prince.

But I sat on as dusk drew down over the city, thinking of the unalterable past—and all my dead.